THE ROCKER WHO LOVES ME

DEMON'S WINGS

USA TODAY BEST SELLING AUTHOR

TERRI ANNE BROWNING

All rights reserved.

1st Edition Published September 2013

Written by Terri Anne Browning

Published by Terri Anne Browning

Edited by: Maxann Dobson. The Polished Pen

Cover Design by Rachel Mizer Shoutlines Designs

Formatting by IndieVention Designs

ISBN-13: 978-1500832292

ISBN-10: 1500832294

10 9 8 7 6 5 4 3 2 1

ALSO BY TERRI ANNE BROWNING

Reckless With Their Hearts (Duet with Anna Howard)
Reese: A Safe Haven Novella

The Rocker... Series:
The Rocker Who Holds Me
The Rocker Who Savors Me
The Rocker Who Needs Me

Acknowledgements

From the very first book, The Rocker Who Holds Me, I've been in awe over how much this series has captured your hearts. I'm still left speechless by how popular The Rocker… series has become. This wonderful journey is so much more special for me with you, the fans, to travel it with me.

As always, I have to thank my husband for putting up with me and my craziness as I write these books for you. Without him there would be no Terri Anne Browning or The Rocker… series. It's his love and support that gives me the confidence and courage to keep doing this for you.

A special thank you to my wonderful BETA readers. They keep me on track and make sure I don't ruin anything for you readers.

What author could live without their editor? I know for sure that I couldn't! Max Dobson is a godsend and I would be grammatically lost without her.

TABLE OF CONTENTS

It looked like the entire trailer park had shown up to pay their respects.

I kept glancing around, taking them all in; anything to keep my gaze from going to the one place I didn't want it to go, yet seemed unable to stop myself from drifting to—the casket and the woman lying there looking so peaceful...

My eyes landed on Mr. Thornton. Jesse's old man was in a pair of faded jeans and a button down shirt that was too tight around his beer gut. His hair was actually combed for once, and it looked like he had taken the time to shave. His eyes were clear, something they rarely were. Mr. Thornton had liked Mom, I guess.

Nik was standing with his mom, really his aunt Sarah who had stepped in when his deadbeat old man died. She looked a little lost. Sarah and Mom had been friends, but we all suspected that there was something wrong with Nik's mom. She had been having horrible headaches lately and couldn't seem to remember things at times.

My gaze drifted past my friend and his mother, landing on random people here and there. A few girls from the west side of the trailer park were grouped together. I had screwed each of them once or twice, they were probably wondering which one of them would be lucky enough to *comfort* me later that night. I didn't want comfort from any of them.

Our landlady was talking to Drake, quietly reassuring him yet again that she wasn't going to kick us out of our trailer. She liked Drake, mostly because he didn't complain when she made him do hard manual labor around the rundown old trailer park that she owned. That old biddy was probably scared out of her mind that we were going to pick up and leave and she'd have to find someone that wouldn't do half the things that my brother did and for more money.

For now we weren't worried about money. Mom had had a sizeable life insurance policy that had covered any possible death. Even suicide…

Something caught my attention out of the corner of my eye and I turned to find Ms. Jameson stumbling in the funeral home's entrance. She had Emmie's arm in a vice-like grip and was dragging the limping little girl behind her. Emmie nearly tripped and tried to hide her grimace of pain.

I wanted so badly to go to Emmie and take her away from that bitch. My brother had nearly gone to jail saving her from one monster, only for her to have to go home and face the one she had to live with every day…

A strong hand landed on my shoulder and squeezed. "How are you?" Jesse's deep voice asked quietly.

I shrugged his hand away. It wasn't that I didn't want the comfort. I just had so much on my mind right now, and a lot of the shit I had tried so hard to forget came flooding back with a vengeance. I shuddered at the very thought of someone touching me…

"I'm fine," I assured Jesse, but of course it was a lie. I wasn't sure how I was, or even how I was supposed to be.

My mom was gone, and it was all my fault. I should never have opened my mouth. I should never have told my mom what had happened or why Drake had done what he had done to Rusty. If I hadn't then she wouldn't have killed her husband… She wouldn't have killed herself!

Tiny fingers gripped my hand. "I'm sorry your Momma is gone, Shane," Emmie murmured in a soft voice.

Some of the tightness around my heart eased as I glanced down at her. For the first time since my world had come crashing down the week before, I felt my eyes burn. I hadn't cried for my mom, or for anyone else. The shock had set in and I was just now unthawing. Crazy enough, it took Emmie to do the unthawing.

I bent down so we were eye level. She was barely nine, but she had seen so much in her young life that she acted years older. I was beyond relieved that Drake had been able to spare her the added nightmares of sexual abuse on top of what she already had to go through daily.

"Thanks, Em." I reached out to push her hair back from her face and saw the bruise on her cheek. It was faded and I figured it was about a week old. Her legs and arms were a symphony of bruises at varying stages, ranging from pale yellow to dark blue and purple. I had to fight with myself every time I saw her like that not to call child services, but I knew that if Emmie was taken from her mom and put into foster care she could possibly end up in a place worse than where she was right now.

"Is it my fault?"

Her whispered question stabbed me in the gut, and I hugged her tight for a long moment before answering. "No, baby doll. This isn't your fault." I pulled back enough to meet her wet, green gaze. "Don't ever think that, okay? You didn't do anything wrong."

After a small hesitation she finally nodded. "Okay."

Jesse bent down and took her hand. "I saw some cookies, Emmie. Let's go get some."

Even though I could hear her stomach growling, Emmie shook her head. "No, I can't leave Shane. He needs me."

Sadly enough, she was right…

Shane

I rubbed the sleep from my eyes and sat up, shaking off the memory of the dream from the night before.

I felt restless, which was nothing new for me. Sighing, I pulled on boxers and a pair of basketball shorts and headed for the kitchen with my shirt tossed over my shoulder. Drake's door was closed and I could hear him snoring as I passed his room. I grimaced, feeling sorry for my brother. I had spent the last two days with Lana while he was chomping at the bit to see her again after so long.

I pulled out a bottle of water from the fridge and chugged half of it before pulling my shirt over my head and searching for my running shoes. I needed a run, something to clear my head of the dream that had haunted me the last few nights. Running always helped me see things clearer.

I took the stairs instead of the elevator so I could warm up. I nodded to the night doorman, who was still on duty, and put my earbuds in as I hit the pavement. Central Park was a few blocks away, and I headed in that direction as I stretched my calves.

The park was pretty dead at this hour, except for the occasional early bird jogger. I ran five miles before I stopped to get another bottle of water. I walked back to the apartment, cooling down but still feeling restless. I knew that it was because I hadn't had sex in three days.

I should just hit up one of my usual clubs, blow off some steam with some stranger. But even as the thought went through my mind, I knew I wasn't going to do that. I didn't want to hit a club. I was tired of that whole scene…And that was just wrong for me. I couldn't remember a time when I didn't want sex. I was used to getting it at least once a day. Three days was a new record for me. Was I getting sick? Fuck, I needed to get my head on straight!

It was still early but I was sure that Drake was up and getting ready for work by now. I wasn't ready to see him again. He would just grill me about Lana and what we had done the day before and what she was doing today. That would just depress us both, and I wasn't in the right frame of mind to add depression to my list of emotions today.

Pulling my iPhone from the strap attached to my upper arm, I brought up Lana's picture and sent her a quick text. ***Bored! Where did you say that gym was?***

I had walked more than two blocks before she responded with the address of the gym that she went to and her roommate worked at. Sighing, I turned my Red Sox cap around and reattached my phone to my arm before turning around. I was going to get a week's worth of exercise in one day.

The guy at the front desk gave me an overly fake friendly smile as I walked through the door. In my tattered baseball cap, worn basketball shorts, and holey T-shirt, I looked like I had about five bucks to my name. From the looks of the place, it didn't cater to the underprivileged.

I liked being comfortable when I ran and didn't give a shit how I looked. If I was doing anything other than exercising, then I made sure I looked good. Emmie and the guys gave me hell over it, but I liked the feel of designer clothes against my skin almost as much as I liked being behind the wheel of a car with some power.

"Can I help you?" Fake Guy behind the counter asked when I just stood there glancing around. From where I was standing I could see the weight room on the second floor, with the treadmills and other cardio equipment to the left of it. The gear I spotted was expensive stuff, and the guys lifting were major body builders.

I pulled out my wallet from the pocket of my shorts and handed over my California driver's license and my Visa. "A friend of mine recommended this place to me," I told the guy. "I'd like to start up a membership."

He took my card and license, frowning when he saw my name. His head shot up and the smile wasn't so fake this time. "Mr. Stevenson, welcome to Fit for Life." He pointed to his name tag like I couldn't see it. "My name is Geoff. I just need you to fill out these papers while I run your card."

I took the stack of papers attached to a clipboard and filled them out, cursing when I realized that half the things on the forms I had no clue how to answer. Emmie knew most of that crap so I didn't have to worry about it. I grimaced, missing Emmie more and more as the days went on.

Emmie was my rock and now I was three thousand miles away from her. For the first time in my life, I was homesick, which didn't make sense when you thought about it. I hadn't even had a real home until last year when we had all settled down in Malibu. But Emmie *was* my home…

I left most of the pages blank, figuring the gym didn't need to know every little thing for them to give me a membership anyway. Geoff gave me my card and license back, along with a keychain card that acted as my pass to get into the gym itself.

"If there is anything you need just let me know. If you want to use our personal trainers they will be wearing blue T-shirts. It's one-fifty for the first session and two hundred after that. Just tell them to bill your account."

I headed straight for the weights upstairs. I had some decent muscles, but nothing like the Hulk-wannabes that were pumping iron like their life depended on it. Veins stuck out from all angles on their spray tanned bodies. As they increased the number of curls they did, the funnier their facial expressions were.

When I was done lifting weights—okay, when I was done people watching—I headed for the treadmills and other cardio equipment. Turning my baseball cap around, I picked up a towel and headed for an empty treadmill at the back of the room. The cardio room was full of more females than males, and I let my eyes wonder as I walked.

There was a cute brunette on a stair-climber who seemed more interested in the early morning talk show playing on the flatscreen television than what was going on around her. Two blondes on bikes were talking about the hair appointments they both had later in the day. The redhead behind them was listening intently as if she was being nosy. All of them were hot, but none of them kept my attention for more than a second.

Sighing, I hopped onto the treadmill beside an older woman with shaved brown hair and some serious muscles that really freaked me out since she was so small. She glanced over at me, nodded her head politely but otherwise didn't give me a second thought. Dressed like I was, it was hard to tell who I was. I also knew that in New York things were calmer than LA when it came to crazy fans.

I pulled my phone off my armband, scrolled through my playlists, and hit play. I had a weird list that included everything from country and pop to metal and techno. I hit the quick start button and turned up the speed so that I was going at a steady pace.

Twenty minutes into my run I got a picture text from Lucy. It was a picture of her and the iguana that Drake had gotten into trouble over getting it for her. Of course Jesse was in the background making a funny face at the huge lizard. Since he couldn't seem to stand the pet, I wondered how he would react if Lucy got her wish and got a snake like she had been asking for. Jesse wasn't exactly a reptile lover.

I slowed down enough to send her a reply. As I finished and hit send, I noticed that the elliptical in front of me had a new occupant. My eyes were immediately drawn to the tightness of her thighs and ass. My mind shut down for half a second, and I had to act quickly or I would have fallen off the damn treadmill.

I hit stop and just stood there, watching female perfection as she mastered the piece of workout equipment. Her legs looked as if they went on forever. Her calves were bare and I noticed a hint of a honey tan to them. I wondered if she was tan all over or if she would have lines from her bikini. My dick twitched at the idea of finding out.

Realizing that I was starting to drool, I closed my mouth and shifted my gaze higher. Her waist was narrow, almost nonexistent. The top she wore clung to her back, and I could see the outline of her sports bra. I couldn't see any tan lines on her shoulders, and of course my dick liked that. Her neck was long, graceful, and exposed with her caramel hair pulled into a ponytail.

As she moved on the elliptical, I saw a tiny tattoo at the base of her neck but couldn't make out what it was. I wanted—needed—a closer look.

Wiping my face with my towel, I jumped off the treadmill and ducked between mine and the scary muscle chick to get to the elliptical next to the hottie. As I stepped onto it she glanced over at me and slowed her pace. She reached for her towel just as I realized who she was.

The two times I had seen her before she had been wearing dark framed glasses, but they hadn't hidden the unique purple of her eyes. She wasn't wearing glasses today, but contacts from the looks of it, which only enhanced the color. For the first time in my life I was hypnotized by a pair of sweet eyes.

"Hey!" She greeted me with a smile that made her nose scrunch ever so slightly at the end. "I thought you said that gyms weren't for you."

I was really glad I had changed my mind! "I got bored," I told her honestly, still captivated by her eyes. "Do you come here often?"

Her brow furrowed for a second and I bit the inside of my cheek. *Really? Had I really just dropped that lame line? I could do better than that in my sleep. Gods! Oh great, now I was falling into Emmie's habit of putting a plural on God. What the hell was wrong with me?*

"I'm usually here when I don't have a job lined up." Harper easily fell back into exercising while continuing to talk to me.

"You're a photographer, right?" I was sure that was what she had told me the first time I had met her. We had a brief conversation while I waited for Lana in the apartment she shared with their other roommates.

She seemed surprised that I remembered. I was kind of surprised myself. I didn't normally remember little details about women, the only exceptions being the ones in my family, and even then I didn't always pay close attention.

"Yeah, I'm doing freelance right now." Her nose wrinkled. "It pays the bills I guess."

"Don't your parents help out?"

The light that had filled those strange eyes of hers dimmed, and I wanted to kick myself. I was really putting my foot in it today. "I don't really talk to my parents unless I have to," she murmured and turned her attention back to the numbers on her elliptical.

Harper

My thighs started burning long before I decided that I had enough of the elliptical. I reached for my towel and wiped the sweat from my brow and upper lip before taking a sip from my water bottle.

Beside me, Shane Stevenson, aka Hot Rocker Man, bounced off his own torture machine like he had another two hours of workout in him. For some strange reason he made me smile.

"So where to next?" he asked, taking his Boston Red Sox cap off and messing with his hair before putting it back on.

"I'm done." An hour was my limit, about enough to work off the desserts I seemed to be addicted to. "I'm hitting the showers."

His face fell and he actually gave me a little pout. "Ah, come on, Harper. Don't leave now."

That pout drew me in and I found myself relenting. "What do *you* want to do?"

Blue-gray eyes darkened and I saw firsthand the look that Lana had warned me about. Shane was supposed to be some bad ass womanizer that could melt the panties of every female with a working libido. I just couldn't figure out why he was flirting with *me*...

"A few things come to mind." His voice was lower, husky.

If I said it didn't affect me I would be a liar. It seemed that my libido worked just fine because I was sure that my panties did melt a little, but I knew better than to take him seriously. Guys as hot as Shane didn't go for girls like me.

I grinned and pushed at his shoulder. "I'm starving. Let's shower and go get some breakfast."

"Or we could do that." He winked and walked with me toward the locker rooms. "I didn't bring anything with me to change into."

"Okay, I'll hurry then. Do you want to go back to your place to change?" I glanced at his shirt drenched in sweat that clung to his hard chest. "Or I could get you something from Linc's locker?"

"Do you think he would mind?" Shane frowned.

I shrugged. "I'm sure he won't, but if you want we can run upstairs to the private rooms and ask him. He and Lana should be close to done by now."

Blue-gray eyes narrowed at my words. "Lana is with Linc this morning?"

"Yeah, didn't she tell you? She and Linc are doing some kind of dance competition. They practice two to three times a week, if not more. Linc pushes her really hard. He has a thing about winning."

Actually, I was sure that Lana was starting to dislike dancing on some levels because of Linc's drive. She wasn't enjoying it like she had a few months ago.

Or maybe it was because Drake Stevenson was in town. Lana had told me about her relationship with the older Stevenson brother, or lack of one if you looked at it that way, so I knew she had to be hurting and conflicted about his sudden relocation to the East Coast.

"Let's go ask Linc." Shane gave me a smile that didn't quite reach his eyes, and I had a sudden crazy thought that maybe Drake wasn't the only Stevenson brother with a thing for my friend.

Why that thought bothered me, I couldn't say. It was almost startling the way my heart felt like it was being stabbed with a stickpin, but I ignored the dull ache and led him over to the stairs. Music was still playing behind the door. Normally, the room was used for the Zumba classes that I sometimes climbed out of bed for.

Shane opened the door and let me go in before him. My roommates were dancing to some Michael Bublé song. It was the first time I actually saw them like this, and I had to say they were pretty amazing. Linc was a big guy, in height and muscle mass, but he looked like he belonged on the dance floor the way he controlled Lana. And Lana looked enthralled as Linc swung her around. The excitement, the happiness I saw on her beautiful face, told me she wasn't completely fed up with dancing just yet.

The couple didn't even notice that they had an audience until the music finally came to an end. When it did Linc started critiquing Lana. "Your leg needs to come up a little more on that last spin, Lana."

"Okay."

"So this is what you blew me off for, sis?" Shane shook his head. "I feel cheated!"

Lana's head snapped up and her face lit up when she saw him standing beside me. "You'll get over it. Wow, three days in a row. I don't think I saw this much of you back in Cali."

"I was bored." He stepped forward and pulled her into a hug.

I watched my friend but there wasn't anything different about the way she looked at Shane than the way she would look at Linc. I shrugged off the idea that the two might possibly be into each other.

"I see you decided to actually get out of bed before noon," Linc commented dryly as he uncapped his protein shake and chugged it.

I grinned up at the man that was my closest friend in the world, second only to Dallas and now Lana. "I thought I would be productive today since I ate half a cheesecake last night. My ass was begging for some help after all those calories."

He rolled his eyes. "You have the best ass in the state, girl."

I rolled my eyes at him, not taking his compliment to heart in the least. Linc was as hot as the surface of the sun, but he was also as gay as they came. "You want to come grab some breakfast with us?"

"I already ate." He tossed his shake back into his gym bag. "And I have a private training session in ten minutes."

What he meant was that he had a private session with some cougar that wanted to look at something pretty while they worked off the lettuce leaves they had forced down the day before. It took hard work to maintain what expensive doctors created. Linc got paid really well for just standing around flirting. The extra tips the cougars slipped him were appreciated as well.

"Have fun." I hugged him before turning back to Lana and Shane, who seemed to be half teasing and half arguing.

"I shouldn't have gone back to your place last night," Lana huffed. "Don't expect it to happen again."

"Don't you like me anymore, sis?" He pouted and I had the sudden vision of sucking on that full bottom lip.

That thought completely tossed me sideways. What the hell was the matter with me? I didn't have random thoughts like that, especially about sex addict rock star playboys. I knew what guys like that were all about, and I didn't need them complicating my life. So of course I did what I do best.

I ran like the hounds of Hell were behind me!

Pulling out my cellphone, I scrolled through the contact list and pulled up Dallas' number. If anyone could understand my reasons for not wanting to even admit to having a crazy attraction for the rocker bad boy it would be Dallas. We had grown up together in the world of modeling, her in front of the camera and me on the sidelines watching my stepsister.

I punched in a quick text for her to call me and get me out of the breakfast I had stupidly invited Shane to.

Shane

I knew she was running as soon as I saw the look in her eyes.

Something about her told me not to let her get away. Maybe I was so bored I needed the challenge. Or perhaps it was because no chick had ever ran from me, like ever. Not once since I had turned fourteen had a female turned me down.

The hottie with the startling purple eyes attempting to turn me down made me smile. I took a step toward her as she answered her phone…

Lana smacked me on the back of the head hard enough to make me stop. I turned around to find the girl I was sure was going to be my sister one day glowering at me.

"No."

I couldn't help raising a brow at her. Lord, she was gorgeous when she was serious. "No?"

"Don't even think about it Shane Mason Stevenson!" she growled low enough that only I could hear her. "She's isn't your type."

I flinched at the use of my middle name. Not even Emmie pulled that particular card on me. I never should have told her my full name! "I don't have a type, sweetheart."

Her brow furrowed even more. "Exactly! So keep your paws off my friend. Or I swear to all those freaking gods that Emmie prays to that I will rip off your man parts."

Sighing, I pulled out my cellphone. "Let's see what Drake has to say about it. Maybe he thinks I should go for it."

I knew I was playing dirty, and the darkening of her amber eyes told me that I had scored one or two this round. "I'll call Emmie," she shot back.

"Emmie?" I snickered. "That all you got, sis? You telling Emmie on me?"

She glared at me for a long moment before her lips twitched and a giggle escaped her. "Okay, I guess that sounded about as mature as a six year old." She poked me in the chest with her finger. It was hard enough to make me grimace. "Be good to Harper, mister."

Oh, I planned on it. I was going to be very good to that mysteriously beautiful female.

Twenty minutes later found me sitting across from Harper at a diner close to her apartment. I had somehow gotten her to agree to still going to breakfast with me. She hadn't wanted to; I'd seen the struggle in those hypnotic eyes of hers as she tried to come up with a better excuse to bail than Dallas needed her to pick up some *girl products*.

It was score one for me when she had finally given in. It was score one for her when she picked a place closer to her apartment than mine. Still, I found myself content to just be in her company as the morning wore on. I wasn't bored when I was talking to her, which was strange because having a conversation with a female that wasn't in my family just didn't happen with me. There was only one thing that I wanted to be doing with a girl that I was attracted to, and sitting down for a chat and a meal wasn't one of them.

It kind of felt like a date, and I was finding it hard to remember the last time I had actually been on one. It might have been when I was seventeen with some girl that I couldn't even remember the name of. She had been particularly easy, and I had scored an hour into the date.

But this was different. I knew I was going to have to pull every trick known to man to get into this girl's panties, and I was actually looking forward to it. For once I wanted the thrill of the chase.

Yeah, I was sure the boredom had fried my brain…

I watched her lick whipped cream off of her thumb and my brain actually shut down for a moment. *Note to self: don't let her eat anything with whipped topping unless I want an aneurysm!* I could actually feel myself panting a little as I continued to watch her eat the waffles topped with the sinful cream and fruit.

She made eating look like a sexy art form. The way she cut her food into small little pieces… The way her eyes went all kinds of dreamy as she took the first bite and savored the taste on her tongue. Even the way her jaw moved in an almost seductive up and down motion as she chewed… Ah, damn!

I had to force my eyes away before she took the third bite or I was sure I was going to pull her under the table and have her then and there! I cut into my steak and eggs with jerky movements in an attempt to take my mind off her and her food. I wasn't even sure if the food I had ordered was actually any good because I was so turned on I couldn't taste any of it.

"So…" I took a deep swallow of my orange juice and attempted to get my body under some kind of control, half fearing I was going to come in the clothes I borrowed from Linc if I didn't. "What made you want to become a photographer?"

"It's something I have always been interested in. I grew up with some of the most talented photographers being a constant in my life. I would sit and watch while they worked their magic behind the lenses, taking the pictures of some really beautiful girls and making them exquisite. I knew that I was never going to be one of those girls in front of the camera, so I thought being the one behind it would be better for me."

She spoke with such enthusiasm that I almost missed it, that soft note of hurt and the pain that darkened her purple eyes. I sat my fork and knife down and just sat there staring at the hauntingly beautiful woman in her faded cutoff shorts, plain tank, and messy bun. How in the fuck did she not know that she was beautiful enough to be in front of the camera? Why would she think something that ridiculous?

It was something I really wanted to find out, but something told me that if I asked she wouldn't tell me. So I stored it for a later time. "You grew up with photographers? Why was that?"

"My stepsister is Ariana Calloway."

I raised a brow because the name sounded vaguely familiar to me. "Should I be impressed?" I asked, not sure if that was the reaction she had been expecting from me.

Harper grinned. "I guess it depends on who you ask. Ariana is still a pretty big deal in Paris and Italy, but not so much here in the states anymore. She's burned too many bridges for anyone to want to work with her. But she is…was…is a supermodel. She was the face for some top names five years ago."

"Ah… Sorry, I still don't know who you are talking about." I opened the internet on my phone and typed in *Ariana Calloway*. There were a handful of pictures that popped up in the image search, and I clicked on the first one to enlarge it for a better look.

Shoulder length dark blonde hair. Cool, almost emotionless blue eyes. Her face was beautiful, but it was a fake kind of beautiful. I wasn't sure if she was still that good to look at under all that makeup. She didn't hold a candle to the beauty sitting across from me destroying my sanity by biting into a cream covered strawberry.

Harper had no makeup on, but she didn't need it. With her purple eyes and crazy long caramel lashes, the Cupid's bow shaped mouth, and striking cheekbones, she had me mesmerized without trying. She had captured my attention the instant I had seen her a few days ago, and she continued to hold it in a way thousands of girls hadn't been able to.

"Beautiful, isn't she?"

I shrugged. "She's pretty."

Harper frowned. "That's it? Just pretty?"

"Okay, she's beautiful. But any decent makeup artist can make anyone beautiful. She isn't all that great to look at." I grimaced. "Sorry if that offends you." I didn't want to push her away by insulting her sister.

"No, that doesn't offend me," she murmured. "I'm just not sure if you are for real. Most guys trip over their tongues when they see Ariana."

"I'm not most guys. I would trip over my tongue to get a taste of you, but I really couldn't care less about your sister."

"Stepsister," she corrected, her tone cool. "And now I know you are not for real." She pushed her nearly empty plate away and reached for her water. "You must have a vision problem."

"No, but now I know why you have to wear glasses." Her brows rose. "Because you're legally blind if you can't see what I see."

She snorted. "Wow, do lines like that really get you laid?"

I couldn't help it. I threw my head back and laughed out loud. "No, sweetness. I don't have to use lines to get laid." They lined up for a chance to warm my bed for an hour or two, but I wasn't going to tell her that. "But with you it's different."

Violet eyes rolled at me, and I swear my dick actually twitched. Fuck. Me.

This was going to be so much fun!

Harper

I had to give it to him. Shane Stevenson was a smooth talker. If I were more naïve I would fall for his sweet talk, but I wasn't naïve. I knew he was playing me.

"So you met Lana at NYU." Shane changed the subject. "What's your major?"

"It was journalism, but I graduated last semester." I was hoping to get a job with a magazine or newspaper, something that was more dependable than the freelance work I was currently doing. At the moment no one was hiring. If anything they were letting people go, so I was lucky to have at least the part-time work.

Shane nodded when I told him this. "I know a few people. Maybe I could help you out."

"No!" I shook my head. "I don't want you to do that. If I wanted an easy in, I could be at Vogue right now. That isn't how I want to start my career off. I want to do this on my own." It was important to me that I do this myself. I needed to know I could do it on my own or all my hard work would be pointless.

And I needed to prove to myself that I didn't need my stepfather's name—or anyone's name but my own—to succeed.

His phone chimed and his lips lifted in a grin as he glanced down at the screen. My eyes were drawn to it and I saw was the name Lulu before he started typing a reply to the text. Another pinprick of pain stabbed my heart and I glanced away.

"One of your adoring fans?" I nearly slapped my hands over my mouth as soon as the words left it. I sounded almost jealous!

Shane continued to grin as he continued to text. "I wouldn't say she is a fan. I doubt her parents let her listen to Demon's Wings music just yet."

My eyes widened. "You have an underage girlfriend?"

"What?" He looked shocked by my question. "No! Of course not. Lucy is only seven! She's Lana's little sister."

I bit my lip, trying not to laugh at his comically stunned expression. "Sorry. I assumed it was one of the many groupies that salivate at your feet."

The way he threw his head back and laughed sent delicious chills down my spine, and I had to avert my eyes from the way his Adam's apple bobbed because it was so damn sexy. As I looked to my left, I found our waitress staring at Shane too. She was eating him alive with her eyes. I realized few women would be immune to this man, and I was starting to think I wouldn't be among those few.

His phone chimed again but I didn't dare look until he grumbled a curse under his breath. I glanced back at him, seeing him pulling his wallet out of the basketball shorts that he had borrowed from Linc. "What's wrong?"

"My brother wants me to come by the studio." All he had to do was glance the waitress's way and she started moving like a moth drawn to a flame. She batted her fake eyelashes at him as he handed her his card. Really? Fake lashes this early? "Thanks, sweetheart."

That was my cue to get going. I should have already been home, maybe even hop back in bed for a few more hours of sleep. But part of me was torn. I didn't want to say goodbye to him yet.

"I need to get home. I have a few pictures I need to edit before I send them to *The Morning Global*." I pulled my wallet from my gym bag sitting at my feet and tossed a few bills on the table for a tip. If he was paying for our food, I was at least covering that much.

Standing, I pulled the strap of the purple and pink gym bag over my shoulder. "Thanks for breakfast."

He slowly got to his feet. The waitress had returned with his card and a receipt. He quickly scribbled his name across the bottom and left it on the table, completely ignoring the girl as she just stood there with her chest sticking out and her lips all pouty. I nearly laughed at the way she was looking at him as I walked past her.

Did girls really think that was sexy? I knew that my stepsister did, and she had caught more than a few guys in her web with that look alone. I thought it looked cheap and more than a little ridiculous.

"Bye, Shane." I called over my shoulder as I reached the door.

"Wait!"

I stopped just outside. The streets weren't as crowded now that most people were at work, but I still had to move to the side so I wasn't blocking the flow of pedestrians walking by.

Shane had his phone in one hand and his wallet in the other as he stepped through the door. "Have dinner with me tonight."

That was not what I was expecting him to stop me for. I frowned at him, sure that he was just playing with me. "Why?"

"Because I like spending time with you. You're fun to hang out with." He pocketed his wallet.

"I like hanging out with you too," I told him honestly. He really was fun to just sit and talk to. Even though I was fighting a seriously big attraction to him, he made me feel comfortable. That wasn't something that I experienced often with a guy.

"Good." His grin was infectious and without hesitating I returned it. "I'll pick you up at seven."

With a sigh I gave in. "Okay. But I'm not dressing up. Can we just grab some Chinese or something?"

"Whatever you want, beautiful. Now give me your number."

Without thinking, I recited the number and seconds later my cellphone chimed with a text. Pulling it out of my back pocket, I found his number and a heart on the screen. "Cute."

He pulled my phone from my fingers and started typing something in. I heard the camera click and figured that he was programing his number and picture ID.

"That's better," he murmured, then pulled me into his arms, turned me around, and snapped a picture of us together with his own phone.

I was sure that I was grinning like an idiot, but that didn't matter. His head was still resting on my shoulder. I turned toward him just a little and his slight scruff rubbed against my cheek. After a moment he finally pulled back, but not before I felt his nose nuzzle against my ear.

"I'll see you at seven," his voice sounded a little deeper, huskier.

I cleared my throat, clearly affected from feeling his warm breath on my neck. "Okay."

Chapter Rock Three

Shane

The line outside the studio was ridiculously long. I saw people with small tents and sleeping bags. Fast food bags littered the ground, and I smelled burgers frying on a tiny portable grill.

I paid the cab driver and stepped out at the front of the long line. Two security guards stood at the doors, along with a thin man with a clip board and a head set. Figuring the little man was in charge, I headed for him.

Of course the first five people in line were female and they noticed who I was even in my hat, sunglasses, and workout clothes. The first one screamed as I walked closer, which sent the rest of the females behind her into a frenzy. The little man frowned at me like I was dirt on his shoes. "You will have to go to the back of the line with everyone else."

"Shane!"

"I love you, Shane!"

The chorus of fans screaming my name was the first thing to alert the guy of his mistake. When I pulled off my Boston Red Sox's hat, he straightened and gave me a warmer greeting. "Mr. Stevenson. We weren't expecting you."

I shrugged. "My brother asked me to stop by."

"Shane!"

I shot the still screaming girls my seductive smile, the one that always got me what I wanted. "Hey, ladies. Are you having a good time?"

"It would be better if you stayed." The second girl in line pouted at me. She was for sure a little hottie, with her long dark hair and blue streaks. She had a body that I could have gotten lost in for an hour or so.

But for once I didn't take up the invite. If anything, I felt a little disgusted as she rubbed her hand over her curves in an open invitation. "Sorry, sweetheart. I have some business to take care of."

The little man spoke into his headset, and a moment later one of the security guards showed me into the building. It was lunch time, or so it would seem. Even though I had just eaten, I was still starving. I hadn't even tasted my breakfast because I had been so into Harper.

The security guard, a guy that looked like he would be right at home in a pro wrestling ring, stopped outside of a door. I nodded my thanks as I walked into the audition room. I took a moment to take in the occupants of the room while they were busy listening to some guy attempt to sing some song he had supposedly written himself.

I was familiar with Cole Steel. He was a legend and I had all of Steel Entrapment's albums. We had even toured with the guy and his band when we first started out. A cancer scare had ended his career, but he was still deep in the music world with other ventures.

Beside of him sat one of my closest friends outside of my band brothers. I loved Axton Cage just as much as anyone in my family and was glad that he had finally seen the light and dumped Gabriella Moreitti once and for all. She had tied him in knots for the duration of their off and on relationship, not to mention made Emmie's friendship with the guy strained because of all the lies she had told Em about Nik.

My brother sat to Axton's right and he looked anything but happy to be there. He was barely paying attention to the guy with the shaky voice, who was just about to piss himself he was so nervous. Drake was doodling something, and I had a feeling it would be something with wings and halos. I felt bad for my brother. He was my hero, the man that had always had my back even at the expense of himself.

The last year had been an up and down struggle for him. Meeting his perfect other half, screwing it up, and going through rehab to get his shit together so he could feel worthy of Lana. And now he was doing a job that I knew he hated because it put him in the spotlight. There was a reason why Drake wasn't the frontman and instead was just the guy with the killer guitar skills, and being front and center was it.

I thanked all the gods that Emmie prayed to everyday that my brother hated that kind of attention. If he didn't he could easily leave Demon's Wings behind and make it on his own. We all knew that. Drake, however, was blind to his talent.

"No," Cole Steel's raspy voice answered, cutting the auditioning hopeful off.

"Sorry, dude," Axton told the guy.

Drake didn't even bother to say anything. He just shook his head at the guy and went back to his drawing.

I waited until the guy left, his head bowed in depression. When the door shut behind him I moved out of the shadows. "Is this what you fuckers do all day? Gods, I would have already started climbing the walls."

My brother's head snapped up and for a brief moment glanced behind me, as if expecting someone else to be with me. Grimacing, I shook my head, knowing that I was just letting him down even before the disappointment flashed in his eyes and he clenched his jaw. I never should have texted him that I had run into Lana at the gym.

"Well, fuck me!" Cole grinned at me as he stood and shook my hand. "How you been, boy?"

At thirty years old, I wasn't much of a boy, even compared to Cole Steel. But having lived hard all his life, I guess he felt beyond his years. "Been livin', Cole. Been livin'."

Drake pushed back from the long judges' table and stood. "I'm starving. Let's go," he muttered.

I ignored his abruptness, knowing he was hating himself and probably aching for a bottle. I was glad that Emmie had found a local AA for him because he was going to need it. "You guys want to join us?"

Axton threw his arm around my shoulders as he and the old man stood, and we followed Drake toward the exit. "Let's get into something we shouldn't tonight."

Normally the offer would hold serious appeal to me. I would even have told Ax to blow off work and we would have found a local sex club and had some fun with a few chicks for the rest of the day. But even as the thought of my typical fun time crossed my mind, a pair of violet eyes eviscerated the images.

"Nah, man," I told my friend as we left the audition room, "I have plans."

Axton stopped and felt my forehead. "Dude, you okay?"

I laughed and pushed his hand away. "I'm cool, man. Just got someone I'm playing with lined up."

"Ah!" Axton grinned. "Well, let me know how she is. I might want a ride or two when you finish with her."

The thought of Axton, one of my closet friends outside of my band brothers, touching Harper made my vision blurry for a moment. I clenched my jaw. "No way! You are staying the fuck away from Harper."

A pierced brow rose at the vehemence in my tone. "Okay, dude. Chill out. Haven't even met the chick. She's all yours."

"Damn right. She's mine."

Harper

After crawling back into bed for a few more hours, I finally forced myself to get up and shower. Pulling my hair into a ponytail, I didn't bother with my contacts, which I only wore when I was either working out or taking pictures.

I had a crazy thought that maybe I should put on some makeup then gave myself a disgusted eye roll in the mirror as I brushed my teeth. I hated makeup and barely knew how to put it on. Ariana had always made fun of me about that. There wasn't much my beautiful stepsister didn't make fun of me for.

Growing up had been pure hell. My mother adored her stepdaughter but barely had time for me. Ariana was the beautiful one, the one that brought in all the money that bought my mother expensive things. I was forced to follow them around the globe as Ariana had made it big in country after country, becoming *the face* for advertisement after advertisement.

At fashion shows I would hide in the corner with a book, trying to become invisible to the gorgeous, mean girls as they prepared to show off their perfection to the masses. With my thick glasses, braces, and flat chest, I would end up the butt of their jokes and bullying if I crossed the other models' path.

Then I had met Dallas and things had started to change. Dallas, more beautiful than any of the models I had ever seen before—more beautiful than even Ariana—wasn't like the others. She looked down her nose at the models, hating every minute she had to be around them. The first time I had met her was the same day she had become my best friend…

"I'm making spaghetti!" Linc called as he passed my room.

I frowned at my reflection in the bathroom mirror and sighed. I loved Linc's spaghetti. It was my comfort food. His special treat for me when my stepsister was in New York, or worse…when my mother was.

If he was making it out of the blue, then it could only mean one thing. One of them was in town.

I rinsed my mouth and wiped away the small white smear on my chin. I wasn't going to worry about them. They were *not* going to get to me this time.

So why were my palms damp? Why was my stomach suddenly cramping with dread?

Muttering a curse that would have had my mother going after me with a brush, I turned away from my reflection and grabbed my phone as I left my room.

Lana was lying on the couch with a pint of ice cream resting on her flat stomach. A can of whipped cream and a bottle of hot fudge sat on the floor beside her. She had a sad look in her amber eyes, and I hated that she was feeling so miserable over a guy. Ever since she had found out that Drake Stevenson was coming to New York she had done nothing but get drunk on Ben and Jerry's.

From the kitchen I could smell that Linc was already putting the sauce together for his spaghetti. Dallas was talking in hushed tones to him, and it was all I needed to confirm that my mother and/or stepsister were indeed in town. Dallas didn't do hushed tones, unless she was trying to protect me from something.

That was why I loved her so much. Because she was so fiercely protective of those that mattered to her.

"Want a bite?" Lana asked as she took another big bite of Chunky Monkey.

I shook my head. "No, thanks. I just brushed my teeth."

"Harp?" Dallas stuck her head out of the kitchen.

I turned to face her. "So… Which one is it?"

Her eyes darkened. "Both."

"What do they want?" It was a really stupid question. They had two reasons for being in New York. One was to get money out of my stepfather. No doubt they were running low on cash now that Ariana wasn't getting modeling contracts like she once had. The second reason was to see me, to make sure I still knew that I wasn't good enough—beautiful enough—to be what my mother wanted in a daughter.

"Monica wants you to have dinner with her and Ariana." Dallas practically spat out the other model's name. Yeah, there was some serious bad blood between my best friend and stepsister.

Normally, even though the whole thing would just make me miserable, I would agree to have dinner with my mother. She was my mother after all. She might not think I was good enough, but I still loved her. But tonight I had plans.

And I wasn't about to ditch Shane in favor of a night of being told repeatedly that I wasn't pretty. Why should I have that fact rubbed in my face when I already knew it, when I could be having dinner with a deliciously sinful rock star?

I glanced down at my watch, a gift from my stepdad the day I had graduated from college. He had been the only one from my family to be there to cheer me on with my friends as I accepted my diploma.

It was already five of seven. Shane would be coming to pick me up soon. "I have plans," I told Dallas.

Dallas raised a brow. I didn't normally make plans without one of my other roommates being involved in them. "Where ya goin'?" Her southern accent always made my heart smile.

"I'm having Chinese with Shane," I told her just as the phone rang.

Lana shot up on the couch, nearly toppling over her drug of choice for the night. "Shane?"

I bit my lip as I turned to look at her. "Yeah… Is that a problem?"

She was frowning, almost lost in her own thoughts as she glanced up at me. After a long pause she shook her head. "No. Have fun."

Dallas had already answered the phone and told Shane to come up. As she put the phone back down, she turned to face me with a wicked look in her eyes.

"There is some kind of justice in all of this." She grinned. "Bitchy and Bitchier are going to shit bricks when they show up and I tell them you went out with one of the hottest rockers in the fucking world!"

I returned her grin, but knew I was going to get an earful when my mother called me later. Picking up my keys, I made sure that my Mace was secure on the key ring before dropping it into my purse. "Enjoy that conversation for me."

"Oh, baby, I plan on it." She reached for my hand and gave it a reassuring squeeze. Dallas wasn't into regular physical contact, mostly because her mother was even worse than my own, so I knew that she was still worried about me. "Enjoy yourself tonight. Seriously, Harp. One of the sexiest men in the world is taking you out tonight."

I rolled my eyes at her. "He's just a friend, Dallas. He's fun company."

"Baby, Shane Stevenson doesn't have girls for friends. Am I right, Lana?"

Lana gave an unhappy sigh. "Yup!"

I laughed. "So what is Lana?" It came out sounding like a joke, but I really wanted to know. Lana and Shane made a striking couple. Sure she was in love with the guy's brother, but it wouldn't be the first time a girl used the brother as a substitute.

"I'm family," Lana informed me with a small smile. "Jesse would kill him if he touched me."

I frowned. "What's the difference in him not touching you compared to Drake?

Lana shrugged. "About two thousand girls."

Well, she told me! I knew Shane was a player... Wait was that the right word for a rock star? A player? Rolling my eyes at myself I grinned. "Well, he's my friend. We got to know each other a little better over breakfast. Trust me, girls. All he could possibly want with me is friendship."

Dallas clenched her jaw and Lana shot me a glare. "Harper..." Lana began but the doorbell cut off her scolding.

I crossed the living room and opened the door, relieved that I had a reason not to hear my friend rant about how beautiful she thought I was. I was sure she needed glasses worse than I did. "Hey!" I greeted him.

He stood there for a moment just staring at me. I felt the heat of his gaze as it traveled down my body, over my barely there chest and wide hips. He spent a little more time on my legs before making the trip back up to my face. I grinned at him as he blinked and took a step closer.

"Hi." His voice was slightly throaty and he paused to clear it. "Are you ready?"

"Of course." I glanced over my shoulder at Lana and Dallas. "See you later. Bye, Linc!" I called.

"Hey, Lana." Shane waved before taking my hand and tugging me out the door.

"Hi!" I heard Lana say as the door shut behind us.

I raised a brow as he pulled me down the corridor toward the elevator. "Are we running late?"

He shook his head, causing shaggy dark hair to fall into his face. "Nope. Just wanted to get you out of there before Lana made you change your mind."

When we were inside the elevator and the doors slid shut, he leaned back against the wall and let out a sigh, as if relieved.

Shane

I have never had a girl make me dumb before. I mean, seriously, words have never—not ever!—failed me when it comes to the opposite sex. But one look at the unspoiled beauty of Harper and I was left with vocals that didn't remember how to work for a moment.

When I had taken her all in, I realized that I was probably standing there looking like a fool with my mouth hanging open and drool running down my chin. Of course she had to smile at me and I lost a few more seconds of brain power. Dammit!

Finally I got it together and pulled her out before Lana started busting my balls over her friend.

Typically when I was in New York I didn't have time to see the sights. When the band had gigs here we didn't have time to go out and explore. I only knew a few good places to eat, and none of those places served Chinese. Thankfully Harper knew of a great place, otherwise I was going to have to do what I always did—call Emmie and ask her.

Normally that wasn't a problem for me.

This time, for some reason, I didn't want to rely on Em for help. I was a grown man. I should be able to do at least a few things on my own. Of course that hadn't been a problem when I had called Emmie earlier that day…

"When we were sixteen Dallas and I ran off for an entire weekend," Harper was saying with an almost impish grin on her face. "It was such a stupid thing to do, but it was so much fun. The first thing we did was stop here and buy enough food to last us all weekend, then we went downtown and got a hotel room for three days. We pigged out on Chinese and vending machine candy until our stomachs ached."

"What happened when your parents found out?"

She shrugged. "My mother hadn't even noticed I was gone. But my stepdad was furious. I wasn't allowed to see Dallas for a month." The look she gave me said that it had been a bad punishment in her book.

"Was it worth it?"

"Hell yeah!" She laughed and it was so infectiously contagious that I couldn't stop from laughing back. "A whole weekend away from my mother? It was paradise."

I wondered about her relationship with her mom, but something in her expression every time she mentioned the woman told me it wasn't the best. "You don't get along with her?" I couldn't help but ask.

She grimaced, her brow furrowing and her lips pursing in the cutest way. "I get along with her. She just doesn't get along with me."

"That makes no sense."

"It's complicated." She pushed an errant strand of silky caramel hair back from her face as she picked up her orange chicken with a chopstick. "I love my mother. When I was a little girl I was sure that she loved me too. But as I grew up, and I didn't look anything like her, she…" She broke off when her cell phone vibrated on the table beside of her eggroll. Instead of answering it, she sent it straight to voicemail. "Speak of the devil," she muttered half under her breath.

For nearly a full minute Harper sat staring down at the phone. The look in her eyes tugged at something deep inside of me, and all I wanted to do was comfort her. Just as I was reaching for her hand her head snapped up and she gave me a smile that didn't quite reach her beautiful eyes. "What were we talking about?"

Realizing that talking about her mother was making her hurt, I shrugged. "You were going to tell me how much you like lemon gelato."

The fake smile was replaced with a real one. "I was?"

I nodded. "And I was about to tell you that I know the best place in this one horse town that serves it."

The smile turned into a full on grin. Gods! That grin was enough to undo me every time I saw it. "I'm not sure if I want lemon. Maybe I want chocolate."

"Because chocolate is boring. Just like vanilla and strawberry are boring. But lemon? With the mixture of bitterly tart and sugary sweet? That's just about perfect."

Her cheeks filled with a pretty pink. I watched in complete fascination as she looked away from me and swallowed hard. My dick pulsed against the fabric of my jeans where it lay against my thigh. Well, shit! Who knew talking about gelato would make me nearly come in my pants?

Her phone vibrated again, keeping me from embarrassing myself in a freaking Chinese restaurant. Muttering a curse she sent the call to voicemail before turning it off and tossing it into her purse. "Sorry. She isn't going to leave me alone."

"It's not a problem for me," I assured her.

"Maybe not, but it is for me." She reached for her water glass and took a long swallow. When she put it back down I found myself unable to look away as her tongue drifted out of that sinfully perfect mouth of hers to lick away a stray drop.

I nearly stroked out just watching her!

Yeah, I was positive. Getting this chick into my bed was going to be so much fun!

She was simply fun to be with. Being comfortable enough with her to find myself laughing and sharing some things that I didn't normally share with anyone outside my band brothers and Emmie, that was just a plus.

After dinner we grabbed a cab and went the thirty or more blocks to get the gelato. When she ordered the lemon with a devilish grin, I nearly came in my jeans for the second time that night. We ate outside at one of the sidewalk tables. The street lights added a kind of mystical appeal to the night.

Halfway through our dessert, Harper pulled her camera from her purse and snapped a picture of me. I wasn't expecting it and for a moment I thought it was actually one of the paparazzi. When I realized it was her I sighed with relief. It wasn't that I was shy of the paparazzi. I just didn't want them disrupting one of the best nights out I had ever had with a girl.

She laughed when she looked down at the camera after taking the picture. "Ah! You're kind of cute."

Cute wasn't exactly one of the words most girls used to describe me, but I liked it coming from her. It seemed sweet and innocent, something I wasn't.

An older couple came out of the shop. It wouldn't have normally caught my attention, but when the man took his wife's hand and linked their fingers, I was unable to look away. The woman smiled up at him, her face still beautiful despite the wrinkles around her eyes and mouth. The look in her eyes was something I had become familiar with over the last year or more. It made me think of Emmie and Layla as they looked up at Nik and Jesse. Even Lana all those months ago before the whole Vegas incident had fucked up her and Drake.

As they passed hand in hand, oblivious to anything or anyone, Harper raised her camera and snapped a few more pictures. "Now that is a Carl and Ellie kind of love."

Her comment confused me. "A what? Who?"

She giggled. "Carl and Ellie."

Had my brain shut down? "Okay, I'm confused."

Another giggle. "It's from a movie. Haven't you ever seen *Up*?"

"There's a movie called *Up*?" I was drawing a blank as I tried to picture what such a strangely named movie would be like.

"It's a cartoon." She rolled her eyes when I raised a brow at her. "Laugh all you want. For me it is one of the best romance movies in the world. The first ten minutes are perfect. Carl loves Ellie from the time he meets her. They grow old loving each other in a way…" She broke off with a sigh. "Never mind. You're right. It's silly."

"It isn't silly." I thought I knew what she was talking about. Hadn't I witnessed that kind of love first hand when Layla and Jesse had first met? "So, you want that kind of love? The 'Carl and Ellie' kind of love?"

She shrugged. "It's something to shoot for."

We sat there talking for another hour before she yawned. I glanced down at my phone and realized that it was nearly ten thirty. Where had the time gone? I wasn't ready to take her home, but knew that I had to. Reluctantly, I stood and we grabbed another cab.

In the dim lighting coming in from the headlights of other cars, I pulled her close and she gave me a shy smile as she rested her head on my shoulder and closed her eyes. I was in a bittersweet kind of limbo for the next twenty minutes. Bitter because I was rock hard and knew that I wasn't going to find any relief with the beautiful creature in my arms. Sweet because it brought a kind of peace in a way that I had only heard my brother drunkenly describe to me what I assumed he had felt when he and Lana had been so close.

In that moment I realized that I wasn't going to be able to go through with the seduction plans I had for Harper.

Not when I was sure that I had found what Drake had been working so hard to get back.

Harper

Strong fingers tenderly brushed across my cheek, and I blinked open my eyes to find Shane gazing down at me with some crazy emotion in his eyes. Crazy because I knew he couldn't be feeling it toward me. I didn't inspire lust in guys.

He cleared his throat. "Hey, beautiful. We're here."

I frowned. "Here?" Turning my head, I found that the taxi had stopped in front of my apartment building. "Oh... Oh!" I pulled away, realizing that I had been asleep on Shane's shoulder...and embarrassingly enough, I'd actually been drooling. Perfect!

With a chuckle, he opened the door and stepped out before offering me his hand to help me. When the taxi pulled away he didn't release my hand, but instead linked our fingers as he walked me inside.

"Do you want to come up?" I asked, reluctant to leave him. He had been so much fun to hang out with tonight, so worth the bitching I was going to hear when I finally turned my phone on and answered my mother's calls.

"I want to..." his fingers tightened around mine, giving them a gentle squeeze before releasing me "...but I don't think I should."

"Oh, okay." I wasn't disappointed. I wasn't!

"Can I see you tomorrow?"

My heart leapt and I had to bite my lip to keep from answering too quickly and sounding like some idiot obsessed and unable to go a day without seeing her crush. Nope, I wasn't crushing on Shane Stevenson. Nope. Nope... Not even a little.

Liar!

"Sounds like fun. Call me and we can make plans... Or you could just come over and hang out?" Maybe he wanted to spend some time with Lana. Damn, there went that pinprick pain to the heart again.

"We can do whatever you want." His smile was adorable, almost shy and a little sweet. Neither of those things were something that I thought I would ever use to describe a tatted up rock star, but they fit nonetheless.

"Okay." I pulled my keys from my purse before taking a step away from him. "See you tomorrow, Shane."

"Harper..?" He paused and I turned back around to face him. His gaze went over my shoulder to where the night doorman was sitting before shaking his head. "Goodnight, beautiful."

The endearment made something tighten around my heart, and I couldn't help the involuntary smile as I pushed the call button for the elevator. It opened immediately and I stepped inside. Shane stood watching until the doors closed between us.

As the elevator ascended to my floor, I beat my head back against the wall of the elevator. Stupid. Stupid. Stupid! Crushing on a guy so far out of my league had to be the most stupid, idiotic thing I had ever done in my life.

Linc and Dallas were still up when I unlocked the front door. They sat on the couch with a bowl of popcorn sitting between them. Since it was a Saturday night, I had been expecting them to be out at a club or some party. As I closed the door behind me, Lana came from down the hall with a phone pressed to her ear.

When she saw me she looked both relieved and concerned. I bit my lip and pushed my glasses up my nose. "What?"

"Nothing," Lana rushed to say. "Nothing... I just wasn't expecting you to come home...so early."

She hadn't expected me to come home at all. "Shane and I are just friends."

"Of course." She nodded. "Sure." She sounded a little confused, but instead of saying anything else, she turned and went back the way she had just came, the phone still pressed firmly to her ear. "Sorry, Layla. Yes, everything's fine..."

I rolled my eyes at my friend as I dropped down on the arm of the couch beside Linc. "What are we watching?"

"Your phone is off," Linc scolded.

I sighed and reached down to pull my shoes off. "Sorry. Mother was annoying the crap out of me so I switched it off. Did you need anything?"

"No. We were just worried." Linc pulled me down beside him and I snuggled close, pillowing my head on his shoulder much the way I had Shane's just a little while ago. His shoulder was wider, more muscular, but it felt uncomfortable. And while Linc smelled deliciously male, it wasn't the scent that I wanted filling my nose. It wasn't Shane's scent...

Well hell!

Harper

I groaned when my phone buzzed on the nightstand beside my bed.

I cracked open one eye to glance at my alarm clock and groaned again when I saw that it was only a little after ten. It was Sunday. I had nowhere to be. No one had a good enough reason to bother me so early!

Ignoring the annoying ringtone, I turned over in bed and used my extra pillow to cover my head until the thing quieted down. When it did I snuggled under my covers and relaxed...

Five minutes later it started ringing again!

Muttering a curse, I blindly reached for the thing to turn it off when I saw that it was from Shane. I shot up in bed, letting the covers fall to my waist. When he said he wanted to do something today I thought it would be later in the day. Rockers liked to sleep until noon, right? With the rumored lifestyle Shane supposedly lived, I was sure he wouldn't call until later tonight. Pushing my sleep tousled hair out of my face, I hit accept and put my phone to my ear.

"Hey."

"Hey, beautiful." His voice was slightly throaty, and I bit my lip to keep from smiling like an idiot. "I'm downstairs. Ready to go?"

"I…Umm…." I grimaced. "I'm still in bed."

"At noon?" He sounded amused.

"No it's not." It couldn't be. Glancing at my alarm clock, I yelped. I guess I had fallen back to sleep and hadn't even realized it! "Oh, it is."

"I tried to call earlier, but it went to voicemail. I can come back later if you would rather." Now he sounded kind of disappointed.

"No!" I jumped out of bed, already pulling fresh underwear out of my dresser. "Give me ten minutes and I'll be ready. Come on up."

"Okay." Was that excitement I heard now?

As soon as he hung up, I tossed my phone on my bed and stripped off my sleep shirt. Tugging on panties, I opened my closet and grabbed the first shirt I saw—a lavender camisole with a built in bra, one of my favorites. Perfect. Reaching for my white skirt, I stepped into it and then added my favorite flip-flops. I rushed through my bathroom routine, brushed my teeth, and smoothed on some moisturizer.

Finally, I snapped my watch into place and left the bedroom I shared with Lana. When I entered the living room it was completely empty. No one was home, not even Lana, and I had to assume she was on campus studying. There was a knock on the door and I saw that it hadn't even taken me five minutes to get ready.

I pulled my hair into a high ponytail as I crossed the messy looking living room to answer the door. Linc and Dallas didn't know how to clean up after themselves on Sunday mornings. Any other day the apartment was spotless, but Sundays? Not so much.

I wasn't prepared for the sight that greeted me on the other side of the door. It wasn't like it was the first time I had seen him for God's sakes. I had spent hours with him just the day before. So why did my breath catch at the sight of sexy as sin Shane Stevenson leaning against the door frame of my apartment? Inked up arms crossed over a lean, muscled chest. He wore a tight white T-shirt, and his jeans hung off of his hips in a way that made my mouth unsure if it was going to fill with saliva or go completely dry.

It wasn't fair that he was so hot. Why couldn't he have been more average looking? Maybe then I would have at least stood half a chance with this guy.

"Like what you see, beautiful?" His voice was still throaty and full of desire. "Because I sure as fuck like what I see."

Heat filled my cheeks and I stepped back, inviting him in while ignoring his question. "Can I get you something to drink? I think there might be some beer in the fridge, unless Linc and Dallas drank it all last night."

Strong fingers gripped my elbow, stopping me from going into the kitchen. Turning, I raised a brow at him. "What?"

His blue-gray eyes were darker than I remembered and trained right on my lips. My heart started racing. "Is Lana here?"

"No, I think she went to campus to study. She has a huge test tomorrow." That was where she normally spent Sundays, whether she had a test or not. She was always studying.

"Good." His voice came out almost a growl.

He moved so fast I didn't have time to react. His fingers tightened around my elbow and pulled my body against his. My small breasts were crushed against his hard chest, and I gasped as his head lowered and he captured my lips. My entire body suddenly felt as if it had been set afire. I moaned, unable to stop the small whimper as it left my slightly parted lips.

He released my elbow, his hands stroking over my body, molding me to him. They came to rest over my hips, pulling me even closer. Those strong fingers gripped my ass through the thin material of my skirt and panties, holding me hard against his lower body. There was no way I could avoid the evidence of his arousal as it pulsed against my stomach. His lips were soft, his tongue hot as it skimmed across my bottom lip in a silent command to open my mouth for him.

When I let him in he groaned, his tongue tangling with my own. My nails dug into his back, holding on to him as I tried to keep up with the kiss. I had no experience with kissing, with anything sex related! But dammit, I was learning fast and liking every second of it. He tasted good, like some exotic honey or nectar. I sucked on his tongue, wanting more of that sinfully sweet taste.

I wasn't ready for it to be over when he relaxed his hold on my ass enough to move half a step back. Slowly, he ended the kiss, his lips lingering for just a moment longer before raising his head a few inches. "I wanted to do that last night but didn't want anyone to see our first kiss."

"That was my first kiss...ever," I whispered.

Shane

I felt like I was going to explode in my jeans.

No kiss had ever affected me like this, not even when I was younger and screwing everything with a vagina that looked at me twice. It was damn near embarrassing, but somehow I kept from nutting off.

I knew Harper was going to be different—special. Last night I had realized that I was developing feelings for her. I hadn't slept much while I tried to determine if I wanted to find out if what I was feeling for her was what Drake felt for Lana or what my other band brothers had found with Emmie and Layla. Part of me had been jealous of their new happiness, while another part had felt sorry for the poor bastards.

After deciding that I at least wanted to see were these crazy ass feelings were heading, I had gone for a run to keep from rushing over to see her. I didn't want to spook her.

But with her whispered words echoing through my head like she had screamed them, I was finding it hard to breathe. Her first kiss. First kiss. First. Kiss.

I had suspected that she wasn't very experienced. Lana had hinted at it, and Harper had shown plenty of signs of it. But she had just basically admitted to being a virgin. Sure, I had deflowered my share of virgins as a stupid ass kid. I had no respect for girls then; I barely respected myself at the time. Fuck, that was still the case!

But not with Harper, dammit!

No matter how badly I wanted her—and it was almost to the point of pain—I was not going to take her virginity. I didn't deserve something that special, not when I was so fucked up. *I would taint her.*

Devastated, I took a step back. Still breathing hard, my body still aching to have her, I pulled away from her. Violet eyes looked up at me with desire until she saw my clenched jaw. "I'm sorry, Harper." I told her and watched her eyes go blank. "I…I can't… This won't work…"

She just nodded and I practically ran from the apartment before I changed my mind. I couldn't destroy her sweetness with my sickness!

As soon as my feet hit the sidewalk outside, I started running. It didn't matter that I was in jeans. All I wanted to do was burn off the frustration making my entire body hurt. My heart felt like someone had stabbed it right in the center. Finally, I had found someone that I wanted for more than a quick fuck, and I couldn't have her!

One of Emmie's gods must really hate me, probably laughing at me right at that moment. I had found paradise and lost it all in the blink of an eye. It wasn't lost on me that the one girl in the world I felt something deep for turned out to be my complete opposite.

I had been screwing every girl that looked interested since I was fourteen, and saying that I had fucked thousands of girls was not an understatement. When Demon's Wings had hit it big, women were lining up for quickies. There were nights when I would start out with one and end the night with two, sometimes three.

Those nights had been fun, but now I just felt sick thinking about them. I felt dirty, unclean, and undeserving of Harper. Sweet, innocent Harper, who had experienced her first kiss with me…

My heart was screaming for me to go back, to take what it now considered as mine, while my brain was shouting at me to keep running. I was only going to cause her pain. All the reasons I shouldn't get close to her or let her love me as I so desperately wanted her to, kept flashing through my mind.

The images had me stopping, my hands on my knees as I tried to catch my breath after the long, demanding run I had just put my lungs through. I was on the verge of puking and tried to get my gag reflux under control.

When the nausea passed I straightened my body out and started running again, needing the physical pain to numb the emotions.

It was more than an hour later before I finally stopped torturing my lungs and legs. Sweat soaked my shirt, and my jeans were beyond uncomfortable to wear. I was somewhere in Central Park, the unrelenting sun beating down on me. Panting, I sat down under a big tree and pulled my cellphone out of my pocket.

Emmie picked up on the third ring. "What's up?" She sounded distracted and I could hear Mia jabbering something in the background.

"Just needed to hear your voice," I told her honestly. I was so homesick for her, especially when I was hurting.

"Everything okay out there?" she asked, her tone concerned now. "You don't sound like yourself."

I didn't want to worry her. She already took care of us and our everyday shit without complaining…much. I was a grown ass man. I could handle my love life on my own. Besides, she probably wouldn't have believed me if I did tell her the truth. "Just finished a run," I told her instead. "How are my girls doing?"

"Mia has a new tooth," Emmie informed me, and I smiled despite the pain still lingering in my chest. "That makes seven now. And she's walking more. I can't keep up with her! Oh, and she said Shay. I'm pretty sure she was saying Shane, so I think she misses you."

"I miss her too. And you." *Especially you.*

Harper

"I hate guys."

I heard her words but didn't raise my head as I continued to edit the batch of pictures I had taken earlier that day for my freelance job that morning. When Dallas started complaining about guys I knew to just nod and agree with her anyway.

"Fucking rock stars."

"Really don't care, Dallas." I didn't mean to snap at her, but if she was going to suddenly tell me that she was sleeping with a rock star, I wouldn't have been able to handle it.

Almost two weeks after my embarrassing kiss with a certain rock star and I was still hurting. I hadn't heard from or seen Shane since that Sunday when he had kissed me and ran. I knew that I wasn't what he went for and he had more than proven that to me.

Of course Dallas went on as if I hadn't even said a word. "Do you know he had the nerve to ask me to be in his new music video?

Like I would ever give him the time of day, let alone prance around like one of his ho-bags in a stupid video!"

I rolled my eyes at her. "If you say so." She was still talking about it, which told me that she secretly wanted to. That was just the way Dallas was. *The lady doth protest too much* and all that bullshit.

"I don't even like his music." Dallas stretched out on the couch beside me, her feet pressed against my thigh as she flipped through the channels without really seeing them. "Demon's Wings are so much better if you ask me."

The mention of that particular band had me grimacing, and I closed my laptop. "So who is it?" I asked. "Some boy band metro sexual guy piss you off?"

"Axton Cage." She said his name with a disgusted twist of her lips, but I wasn't blind to the interested light in her baby blues. "He is such a douche."

I raised a brow at that. "You met Axton Cage?"

"Yup. When I went with Lana this mornin'. Shane called to invite her to watch the auditions. She already leave for her date with the Demon?"

"Shane?"

"Drake," Dallas corrected, a smirk on her face. "Bettcha ten bucks she doesn't come home tonight."

I rolled my eyes and pushed my glasses up on my nose. "No deal. We both know that she isn't coming home." It wasn't that Lana was easy. She was just so in love with the guy that she wouldn't be able to turn him down if that was what he had in mind. And if he was smart, he would definitely have *that* in mind.

"How did your shoot go this morning?" she asked, apparently done with her *rock star* rant for the moment. "You never said who the job was for."

I couldn't help but grin. My personal life might not be the greatest at the moment, but I was thriving in my career. "It was *Rock America*. They needed someone to cover a story and take some pictures. I sent them my portfolio before graduation and didn't think I would ever hear back from them. I already emailed them my article and the pictures I thought worked best and the editor was in love with my work!"

"Harp, that's amazeballs!" Dallas nudged my leg with her foot. "We need to celebrate."

Any other Friday night and I would have turned her down. I knew from experience that her idea of celebrating was going out to a club. Clubs just weren't my scene, but tonight I needed to go out and drink away the depression I had been feeling.

I surprised Dallas by saying, "Okay, make me beautiful."

Blue eyes narrowed on me. "That doesn't take much effort, babe. But if you want me to, I can do your makeup."

Two hours later we were in the middle of *Club 101* and I was halfway into my third margarita. I started to feel the effects of the tequila in a good way and danced with Dallas in ways I never would have done if I were completely sober. Laughing, I tossed back the last of my drink and hugged my friend close.

"You are such a light weight." Dallas teased as she took my glass from me. "You need water before you get another round."

With a pout, I followed her to the bar and downed half a glass of ice water before she would let me have a shooter. Of course she was on her fourth beer—and who knows what number of shooters— and wasn't even feeling the effects yet. Dallas had been drinking since she was twelve as a way of coping with her mother.

When our pink lemonade shooter was set in front of us, Dallas picked hers up and lifted it in a toast. "To deserved new beginnings. If that editor for *Rock America* has any sense, they will snatch you up."

"I'll drink to that!" I tossed the shooter back, licking my lips as a drop clung to the corner of my mouth.

"It's about time he got here." Dallas pointed toward the entrance, and I followed her gaze to find Linc coming in. "Who's that with him?"

I frowned, not having noticed that Linc wasn't alone until she had pointed it out. The club was so crowded it was hard to make out who was with whom. Of course it was hard to miss Linc as tall and broad as he was. With the guy behind him just a few inches shorter and a good twenty pounds leaner, I didn't see him until it was too late.

Dressed in designer jeans that looked like they had been made specifically for him, a shirt that had some MMA fighter's logo on it, and his hair styled in a I-don't-care-and-I-still-look-sexy-as-hell kind of mess, Shane made my mind go blank for a second.

And then the kiss came back to haunt me.

I closed my eyes as the remembered embarrassment washed over me. I turned away, not ready—really would I ever be?—to come face to face with the man that had given me my first knee weakening kiss before running off like the hounds of Hell were right behind him.

Of course I couldn't just ignore him. Linc, and especially Dallas, would know something was up, and I didn't want to tell them how stupid I'd been in thinking for all of five minutes that I had a chance with someone like Shane. So when the two men reached us, I gulped down the last of my water and pasted on a smile before turning around.

"Hey, stranger," I greeted him. "It's been a while since we saw you."

Shane smiled but it didn't quite reach his eyes. Was it so hard to be around me now? It wasn't like I was going to claw his eyes out or anything. He couldn't help that he didn't want me. "Hey, beautiful."

"Poor bastard was waiting in the lobby when I got home," Linc said, turning from the bar with two beers. Handing a Corona over to Shane, he laughed. "His brother kicked his ass out."

Dallas snickered. "Told y'all she wasn't comin' home tonight."

"I'm not going to complain. They should never have been apart in the first place." He took a long pull off his beer. His eyes kept drifting to me, and of course he caught me staring each time.

Grimacing, I turned around to order another shooter…

"Shane!"

We all turned when a girl screamed his name. "Shane Stevenson!" she squealed, running up and throwing her arms around his neck. Her lips covered his before I could even figure out what was going on.

He didn't struggle, but he wasn't exactly holding on or kissing her back. I figured she was some drunk college girl that had spotted the rock star and thought she would say hello…or whatever!

"Yo, bitch!" Dallas grabbed the drunk girl by the hair and pulled her back. "My friend isn't interested. Go suck face with someone else."

The drunk girl took Dallas in, sizing her up. If she was smart she would walk away. Dallas was not someone to get into a catfight with. I have seen her pull a girl near bald and scratch up her pretty face firsthand. She fought dirty and didn't care who knew it. The other girl only glared at Dallas for a moment, noticing her tattoos and piercings and determined that she wasn't sober enough to mess with my friend.

Shrugging, the drunk girl walked away without a backwards glance.

"Another round!" Linc called to the bartender with a laugh.

Shane

The past couple of weeks had been anything but easy for me.

I tried everything possible to forget about Harper Jones and the kiss that nearly brought me to my knees. And I mean *everything*!

After calling and talking to Emmie, I had felt more grounded. Emmie always had that effect on us all, but for me especially. Once I had gotten my shit together, I had took Axton up on his offer of hitting one of the many clubs that every major city hosted.

Two hours into a foursome and I was feeling more sick and nauseated more than anything else. There I was with two blistering hot chicks, ready and openly begging me to fuck them hard, and all I had felt was dirty and ready to vomit. Axton had laughed it off, telling them that I had some bad sushi. I took the excuse and ran... Literally. I grabbed my shit and got out of there fast.

One kiss. That was all it had taken for Harper to leave her mark on me. I wasn't fit for anyone else. The thought of some other female with her hands on me made my stomach roll and I broke out in a cold sweat.

Still, I hadn't been ready to give in. I still thought I was going to taint Harper with the things from my past.

Unable to do what I normally did, which was fuck everything in sight with a vagina, I started running more and more. Sometimes I would even go to Fit for Life in the middle of the night and just run on the treadmill for hours. When that didn't work, I would hit a bar or club and drink until I couldn't remember my name.

The second morning I woke with a hangover to rival any that I could remember my brother having, I realized that I couldn't let myself go down that road. Not only was it not where I wanted my life to end up, but I had to respect Drake enough not to do that shit when he had come so far after his own battle with the bottle.

Yesterday I had finally faced the truth. No matter how scared I was of my past and sullying Harper with it, I wasn't strong enough to give her up.

When Drake had called earlier tonight and told me to stay out of the apartment for the night, I had gone to the one place I wanted to be more than anywhere else—to Harper's. Of course she hadn't been home and I'd been a chickenshit, scared that if I called or texted her she wouldn't answer.

Not that I could blame her. I kissed her and ran. She probably thought I wasn't worth her time, and she would be so right.

Linc had saved my ass, getting home just when I was ready to give up and go to the gym for a few hours. When he invited me to come with him to the club, where Dallas and Harper were waiting for him, I had rushed to accept.

Now, with the taste of some other girl's lip gloss and smoke from whatever she had been smoking filling my mouth, I was ready to grab Harper and rush her out the door. Linc handed me another beer as Dallas moved in front of me as if guarding me from other drunken girls ready to attack.

Swallowing half of the Corona to get the bitter taste of the girl out of my mouth, I took the time to look Harper over. Her makeup was meticulous, highlighting her eyes and making her lips look so damn kissable and plump. With her short skirt and a top that barely covered her tits, she looked smoking hot.

I didn't like it. I wanted *my* Harper standing in front of me. The unspoiled beauty that didn't need thick makeup or club clothes to make my dick hard. I wanted to drag her to the nearest bathroom, wash that shit off her face, and then kiss her until neither one of us could think straight.

The guarded look in her violet eyes told me that wasn't going to happen.

"Have that happen to you often?" Linc asked with a grin as he handed the girls their drinks, something pink and girly.

I shrugged, not wanting to admit that it happened more often than not. A month ago I probably would have been deep between that girl's legs in some dark corner of this club. "Let's dance." I looked right at Harper as I suggested it.

"Yes!" Dallas pushed Harper at me and grabbed Linc's arm, already pulling him toward the dance floor. "Come on, Harp. I love this song!"

Harper didn't even look up as she turned to follow her friend. Sighing, I followed, knowing that I had a lot to make up for.

The dance floor was pretty crowded. For once I was glad for it. It meant that Harper had no choice but to dance close. I grinned as I pressed into her back. She shot me a frown over her shoulder before turning back to Dallas who was grinding against Linc as the music quickened in tempo. Whomever the DJ was, he knew his stuff because the music was freaking awesome.

When Harper relaxed a little against me, I didn't waste time taking advantage and twisting her around to face me. "We need to talk." I had to lower my head to speak loudly into her ear. This close, I could smell her perfume. Had a girl ever smelled as good as Harper?

Her brows rose. "What about?"

"Us."

She laughed. "Sorry, I thought you said *us*."

"I did." I gripped her hips and pulled her closer when two girls cut between us, and Dallas and Linc. When they were gone I didn't release her, liking her against me far too much. "I want to be with you, beautiful."

"What?" She looked confused.

I shook my head. It was too loud in the club to have this conversation here. "Just dance with me!"

Laughing, she rolled her violet eyes at me. "Whatever you say!"

For the next two hours we had a good time. It was fun watching Dallas and Harper—and yeah, even Linc—as they danced around me. A few girls tried to come up to our group, each with their drunken gaze on me. I was the notorious one of Demon's Wings now that Nik was out of commission as a soon to be married man. Of course I was the more notorious one to begin with. Even before he had gotten his head out of his ass and admitted to Emmie that he was in love with her, he hadn't cared as much about getting laid as I had.

Now that I wasn't interested in that whole scene, I realized how annoying those girls could be.

But with Dallas around those girls didn't get far. I decided after the third girl was royally bitched at that it was nice having that country girl around.

"That's right, bitch!" Dallas yelled at the latest bottle blonde tried to squeeze between Dallas and Harper to get to me, "Keep walkin'. He doesn't do nasty!"

That got her an ugly glare over the bottle blonde's shoulder, but she kept walking all the same.

Beside me, Harper was giggling as she leaned against Linc while she sipped her Cranberry and Vodka through a little black straw. Gods, she was cute with her makeup smeared every which way from sweating for the last two hours. She was pretty tipsy and kept tugging at the hem of her skirt in an attempt to pull it down.

Dallas turned back around, nearing the drunk line herself, and high-fived Harper. "You are so going to fight someone tonight if you don't watch," Harper warned.

Dallas shrugged. "Bring 'em on!"

Despite her warning, Harper didn't seem all that worried about the possibility, and I figured that she didn't really need to be. There was something about Dallas that just screamed *"don't mess with me."* The mixture of ink, piercings, and maybe even the set of her shoulders hinted at how tough she was.

"Okay, you sexy bitches." Linc took hold of Harper's hand before reaching for Dallas. "I have to work early. Let's pay our tab and go home."

"I'm having a good time," Harper complained as Linc pulled her through the crowd toward the bar. "I don't wanna leave yet."

I couldn't help grinning at how young she sounded when she was half-lit. "You keep up with those shooters like you have been all night and you're going to need my hangover bucket." Linc sounded like a scolding parent as he tugged the girls through what looked like a bachelorette party.

I didn't give any of them a second glance as I followed close behind Harper. "You ruin all the fun, Linc."

"I know, sweetheart. I know."

"Oh. My. God!"

As soon as I heard the squeal I knew it was coming. I knew that one of the girls from the bachelorette group had realized who I was. Most girls that knew who I was knew my reputation, so I wasn't at all surprised when someone jumped on my back and started sucking on my neck like a vampire in heat. "Fuck me in the bathroom, Stevenson!"

My new friends turned and stared, mouths gaping, at the sight of some strange girl basically humping me while her teeth bit roughly at my neck. Scared I would hurt her if I tried to untangle her I just stood there, silently begging my friends for help.

"What the fuck!" Dallas exploded and tore the other girl off my back.

Not expecting the interruption, the girl's teeth scraped across my neck as she was jerked back. I yelped in pain and touched my neck, feeling a few drops of blood bead on my skin. Linc pushed past me, and I realized that Dallas had the drunk girl pinned to the floor, and hair was flying.

Bright red hair that sure as hell didn't belong to Dallas!

Harper

I didn't know whether to laugh or help Dallas out as she ripped the drunk girl off Shane's back. Of course I was surprised that none of the other girls with the bachelorette party didn't step in to help the drunk girl. Instead, they just stood back and watched the show, as if in shock that it was actually happening.

It was seriously hilarious, especially as Shane was helpless to do more than stand there and watch. Then I noticed the wound on his neck. "You're bleeding!" I exclaimed, reaching up to touch the spot on his neck that the girl had bitten.

He winced and then paled when he saw the little smear of blood on my fingers. "Tell me that's my blood, Harper. Tell me it's mine."

"It's yours." I rushed to assure him, worried when he turned green right before my eyes. "I swear."

"Okay, Dallas!" Linc was attempting to pull her off the other girl, who was screaming for help. "Let the poor girl go."

"Kick her ass!" I yelled down at my friend. "He's bleeding!"

"You skank!" Dallas shouted in the drunk girl's face. "You hurt my friend!" With her fingers tangled in the girl's hair, she shook her head like a rag doll's while she screamed obscenities at her. Her lip was bleeding from one of the punches Dallas had landed on her face, not to mention the hand prints on either side of her face from the bitch slaps that my friend had dished out.

Dallas had a hell of a bitch slap. Her hand print would be on that girl's face for up to a day before it started to fade.

"Dallas, that's enough." Linc lifted her with little effort, her fists clenched around handfuls of bright red dyed hair. "The bouncers are going to throw us out. Let her go. Dallas!"

Dallas struggled to get free so she could finish what she had started. Spitting curses that I wasn't sure I even knew the meaning to, she was a sight to behold. I loved how fierce she was. Finally, Linc tossed her over his shoulder and headed for the bar.

Shane grasped my hand and we followed after them. When I turned my head to look back at the girl, she gave me a pissed off look, and I grinned and shot her the finger. "That's what you get, bitch!" I called back to her.

"Gods, you two make me homesick!" Shane laughed as he pulled me through the crowd.

"Why's that?" I asked, turning back to face him.

"Dallas reminds me of Em."

I frowned, trying to remember who that was. "Oh, yeah. The chick that called and chewed Lana out back in May for not going back to LA."

Shane grimaced. "Yeah, that's her."

"She doesn't like Lana much, does she?"

"She loves Lana. She just loves Drake more." He pulled his wallet out and handed the bartender a bunch of bills, covering all of our tab. "She's spent most of her life taking care of him, of us all really."

I could understand that, I guess. "So, she's like your sister or something?"

"Yeah, that's exactly what she is. My sister." He gave my fingers a squeeze and then pulled me toward the closest exit.

Linc already had a taxi waiting for us when we reached the street. Dallas sat in the back sulking. "I wasn't finished with that bitch."

"Ah, poor baby." Shane patted her knee as he scooted in and pulled me close as Linc shut the door and hopped in the front. "Thanks for defending my honor, sweetheart."

Dallas bit her lip to keep from laughing. "Sure."

I couldn't hide my snicker as the taxi pulled into traffic. "Dallas, you just defended the biggest male slut in the rock world. That's brave."

"God, Harper. You are so lit!" Linc called from the front seat.

"Hey!" Shane pinched my side, making me squeal and giggle. "I'm a reformed male slut, thank you."

"Oh, sorry. Reformed male slut. How long has it been since your last fuck?"

Linc was right. It had to be the alcohol making me run off at the mouth the way I was. Normally words like *fuck* just didn't cross my lips.

"A little over two weeks."

"Holy shit!" I cried. "That's got to be a record for you. Are you sick or something?"

Blue-gray eyes narrowed at me in the dim light of the taxi. "Or something."

Yeah, the alcohol had hit me hard, and now I was seeing things. Shane Stevenson was not looking at me as if he wanted to devour me. It just wasn't possible after his kiss-and-run just a few weeks before. The arm that he had around my waist pulled me closer, and I felt a little dizzy as he lowered his head and nuzzled my ear. "Definitely something, beautiful," I thought I heard him whisper.

"Well, that was one bachelorette party those girls won't forget," Linc commented, breaking the spell Shane had suddenly put me under. "Hope the wedding isn't tomorrow, or the bride will have a half bald bridesmaid."

It didn't take long before the driver pulled in front of our apartment building. Shane's hand lingered at the small of my back as we followed Linc inside. The night doorman was leaning back in his chair behind his desk when we walked in. I waved at him.

"Hey, Curtis!"

"Evening, Miss Jones."

The elevator opened as soon as Dallas pressed the button. We rode up to the twelfth floor in near silence. Dallas was starting to feel the effects of her fight and the alcohol and was leaning against Linc as she closed her eyes. "Bed," she grumbled as soon as we entered the apartment moments later.

"Night, Dallas," Shane called after her retreating back.

"I'm going to turn in too," Linc said as he headed toward the hall that led to our bedrooms. "I have to be at work early."

"Dude, it was fun tonight. We'll have to do this again."

Linc laughed. "Yeah, I had a good time."

I flopped down on the couch, the remote already in my hand. When Linc's door slammed behind him, Shane sat down beside me and snatched the remote from me. "How many channels does this thing have?"

I shrugged. "Linc ordered the whole package, so there is plenty to choose from." When it landed on some sports network, I grunted. "No, no, and no. If you're staying I'm not watching stupid sports."

He sighed and switched it to a chick flick on one of the movie channels. "How is this?"

"Nope. Do you want to make me gag?" I took the remote back and looked through the menu for a few moments before settling on a late night horror movie. It was something that Lana and I had in common, our love for scary movies. "I love this part."

"I knew I loved you." He draped his arm along the back of the couch.

"Shh, this is the best part."

"Of course it is," Shane muttered and reached for my leg to pull my feet up into his lap. I shot him a curious look, but he just pulled off my flats and started rubbing my aching feet.

My eyes rolled back in my head, and I couldn't help the small moan that escaped as his thumb put pressure right in the arch of my left foot. "Oh… Oh that feels wonderful."

"You like?" His tone was throaty, but I didn't open my eyes as I nodded. "Should I stop?"

"Stop and I will hurt you." His chuckle followed my threat, and I peeked through my lashes to find him leaning just a little closer. My heart started racing. Memories of our kiss flashed through my mind, and my lips started to ache for a repeat.

Then the sweet memories faded and the hurt poured back in when I remembered him running out when it had just started to get good. Pulling my feet away, I sat up straighter. "Th-thanks," I mumbled, forcing my gaze back to the television.

"What's wrong?" he demanded, reaching for my hands, but I pulled them away. "Harper?"

"I don't know how to play your games, Shane," I told him honestly, forcing myself to meet his gaze. "I'm not sophisticated enough to even understand the rules. One minute I thought we were friends, then you kissed me…" I sighed. "And then you just ran off and I didn't hear a word from you for almost two weeks. Now you're back, and tonight was fun. Really, really fun. I loved dancing with you and hanging out. But just as friends. Nothing more."

Blue-gray eyes darkened as he listened to me. "I'm sorry I ran after that kiss…" He scrubbed both hands over his face. "You scared the hell out of me, beautiful. I won't lie. I've been around. So try to understand when I tell you that no one—*no one*—has ever made me feel what you make me feel. It was almost terrifying, and I ran away like a coward. I'm sorry, baby. It's not going to happen again."

Yeah, okay, so his words kind of took my breath away. If it was a line, then it was a really amazing line. But I wasn't willing to fall for it. If he was a coward, then so was I, because I wasn't willing to risk my heart with him…not when it was half involved already.

"I just want to be friends, Shane."

The rocker just sat there, frowning at me in the dimly lit living room while *House on Haunted Hill* played in the background. I felt like he could see into my very soul the way he was looking at me right then. After nearly a full minute, he finally nodded.

"Okay. Friends, for now." I opened my mouth to tell him that it was for always, but he cut me off. "I'll make you change your mind, beautiful."

I knew that I had fucked up. Running away never solved anything. I knew that. Now I had a lot to make up for, and I was going to do just that.

So I watched stupid *House on Haunted Hill* with Harper until she fell asleep with her feet in my lap. Picking her up, I realized that she barely weighed anything at all. I carried her to bed and tucked her in. Of course I couldn't resist brushing a kiss over her cheek before leaving her.

By the time I got home it was nearly three in the morning. The apartment was quiet and I stopped dead in my tracks when I saw the clothes spread across the living room. Grinning, I tossed my keys aside and headed for my room. It was about time Drake got what he deserved. I was thrilled for my brother and Lana.

Of course he wasn't so thrilled with me when I had to interrupt them the next morning because Layla kept calling Lana's phone. As soon as I gave her the phone, I made a run for it. No way did I want to be around when they finally came out of that bedroom.

My day was spent making phone calls from a coffee shop I knew Harper liked. I had grilled Lana about her for the last two weeks and knew her likes and dislikes by heart now. As I surfed the net on my phone, I realized I was acting a little stalker-ish and grimaced. Great, now I was turning into a psycho!

Of course that thought went flying out of my head when I saw her come into the shop and head straight for the counter. Picking up my half empty cup of triple espresso—which had nothing on Jesse's special blend—I tossed the now cold drink and got in line behind Harper to order another one.

While she spoke to the skinny kid, ordering some kind of girly mocha with extra whipped topping, I took my time checking out the view from behind. Gods, but I loved her ass. The leggings she was wearing outlined it perfectly, and I had to ball my hands into fists to keep from reaching out to cup those sweet hips.

She was wearing running shoes and a tank top, so I had to assume she was planning on a trip to the gym. It was after one, which didn't surprise me. Lana had told me that my girl liked her sleep, and I had kept her up pretty late the night before.

When she started to pay for her coffee, I stepped forward and took care of it while ordering my own with some pastries. I hadn't needed Lana to tell me that Harper had a sweet tooth. After paying, I turned to face the quiet girl standing beside of me.

Was it me or was she more beautiful when she was trying to be mad. "I can pay for my own coffee, Shane."

"No one said that you couldn't, beautiful. I just wanted to buy my *friend* something to drink." I leaned closer to her as I said the word *friend* and enjoyed the sight of pink flushing her cheeks. Of course I got a hint of the perfume she was wearing and nearly groaned as it had an effect on my dick.

The barista put our cups down in front of us along with the dish of pastries. I sent the kid a smile as I picked up our order and led her toward the table I had taken up for most of the day.

I sat the coffee down and pulled out a chair for her. Other than a few times for Emmie, I didn't think I had ever done that for a girl before. Harper didn't look impressed, though. She just sat down and snatched up one of the cherry filled pastries. "I really don't have time for this."

"What's so important that it can't wait twenty minutes while we share a snack?" I asked as I sat down across from her so I could see her eyes. Gods, I loved her eyes!

"I'm meeting Cecil at the gym for some racquetball."

My entire body tensed up as the name of another man left her lips. "Who the fuck is Cecil?" I demanded before I could stop myself.

"My stepdad," she said with a roll of those gorgeous eyes.

"Oh..." Dammit! Now I sounded like an obsessive asshole. Girls didn't like shit like that, did they? Emmie and Layla didn't like it much, or at least they said they didn't. Was it some kind of reverse psychology and they really did?

A small smile teased at Harper's Cupid's bow, but she didn't chastise me. "Cecil is kind of the only family I claim. He wanted to adopt me, but my real dad wouldn't let him."

"Why not?"

"Because he's a control freak." She grimaced and took a sip of her coffee. "He and my mom are a lot alike in that area."

"So you and your stepdad get along?"

"Oh yeah. He and I are so similar, just like Ariana and my mom. Dallas used to joke that we got switched at birth." Her grin was adorable and I wanted to sit there and stare at it for hours. "We don't get to see each other much these days. He's been so busy with work, and I've been trying to find a full-time job. But we try to get together at least once a month for racquetball or dinner."

"Then you should get going." I didn't want her to go, but I hated for her to miss out on time with her stepdad.

She glanced at the watch on her left wrist. "I still have a few minutes. He's always a little late anyway."

I would take anything she was willing give me. Minutes, hours, days. I wasn't going to ever turn that down. "How is Dallas feeling this morning? Sore from the fight?"

Harper laughed. "Apparently, that drunk girl got a hit or two in last night. Dallas has a bruise on her right cheek. It really makes her dimple stand out."

"Now I feel bad."

"Why?"

"She was fighting because of me. I got her hurt." I hated that. Don't get me wrong. Catfights were hot as hell, but I didn't want my friends hurt because of me.

Harper shrugged it off. "Dallas was half-drunk. She's always looking for some kind of drama when she gets like that. That's why I make sure Linc goes out with her when she wants to go clubbing."

"Really? Sweet little Dallas likes drama? I never would have assumed that of her." Harper's giggles were sweet to listen to. I wanted to capture it so I could listen to it forever.

Harper

I had to admit that Shane could easily make me laugh. I loved that about him.

When it was time for me to go, I was reluctant. So of course the words slipped out before I could call them back. "Want to come play racquetball with me and my stepdad?"

His eyes widened as if my question startled him. "You want me to come with you? Meet your stepdad?"

"Yeah. It will be fun. You're really athletic so you should be able to keep up with him better than I can."

He glanced down at his gray T-shirt and basketball shorts. I liked them on him better than the club clothes he'd had on the night before. It hid more of his sinfully sexy body, and I could think easier like this.

"Okay."

I wasn't sure how Cecil was going to react to Shane. I had never introduced him to a guy that I liked before. He was protective of me, more so than he had ever been of Ariana. But then again, he knew that no matter what he said or did, Ariana would do what she wanted regardless.

When we got to Fit for Life, Cecil was just warming up. When he saw me his face lit up. I threw my arms around him, and he hugged me tight. "There's my girl!"

When he released me, I stepped back and gave him a once over. He was tall with jet black hair, sprinkled with gray, and blue eyes. He was still a handsome man even in his late fifties. Ariana had gotten a lot of her features from her dad. Sadly enough, she had gotten her personality from her mother, who had been best friends with my mom until her death.

"You look tired," I scolded. "Don't you sleep enough?"

"I've been in meetings for over a week straight, baby cakes. The new takeover is draining this old man." His deep voice sounded a little hoarse, and I wondered if he was getting sick or if he had started smoking again.

"Cecil…" I started to ask which it was when he glanced over my shoulder and noticed Shane.

Cecil's blue eyes narrowed, taking in the rock star. "Who's this?" Although his eyes weren't exactly friendly, his tone was. That's what I loved about my stepdad; he wasn't readily judgmental about people. He gave them a chance.

"This is Shane Stevenson. He plays the bass for Demon's Wings."

"Ah, Lana's brother-in-law's band." He had met and liked my new roommate on sight. Cecil stepped forward and offered Shane his hand. "Good to meet you, Shane."

Was it just me or did Shane look nervous? I bit my lip to keep from grinning at that crazy thought. "Good to meet you too, sir." Shane said as he shook the older man's hand.

"Do you play?" Cecil asked, motioning to the racquetball room in general.

Shane shrugged. "A little. Haven't had much time for it in the past, though."

"Well, now is as good a time as any to start, son."

Twenty minutes into our first game and I was sitting in the corner, winded and watching the two men playing like pros. For

Cecil, that was the truth. He had been playing for most of his life. Shane, on the other hand, had openly admitted to not playing much racquetball. He was naturally athletic and after stumbling for a few minutes, he'd picked it up like he had been born playing.

He sure was giving my stepdad a workout. Cecil was enjoying the challenge, laughing and teasing Shane. I could feel him warming to the rock star with each passing minute. Shane seemed to be having a good time too. He had relaxed considerably since we had first arrived. I thought it was adorable that he had been nervous, if that really had been the case.

Half an hour later and the men were shaking hands. Cecil had won, but I wondered if Shane had let him have the victory. Actually, I was sure of it when Cecil ribbed him about it and Shane caught my eye and winked. My heart melted a little, loving that he had taken my stepfather's feelings into account like that.

"Loser has to buy dinner," Cecil informed him, dropping his racket into his bag before wiping his face with a towel. "I'm starving. Kicking your ass has given me a big appetite."

"Absolutely," Shane readily agreed. "I have a change of clothes in my locker upstairs. Beautiful, do you need to go home and change?"

There he went again, calling me beautiful. I didn't know if I liked it or not, but I wasn't going to ask him to stop. When he used that term of endearment, I almost felt like it was true. "No, I have a change of clothes in my locker too."

Cecil rubbed his hands together. "Good! Let's hit the showers."

Dinner was maybe one of my favorite meals ever that evening. Shane took us to one of Manhattan's exclusive restaurants. We didn't have to wait to be seated, and our table was one of the best in the entire dining room. I guess Shane was trying to impress Cecil, and he did that in abundance. My stepdad might not be a snob, but he had expensive taste. He had been born into the world of money and had more than tripled his family's fortune since taking over for his father twenty years ago.

I wasn't exactly comfortable in the big money world. I didn't like that lifestyle and had witnessed that it wasn't exactly the road to happiness. But with Shane there, looking down his nose at all the money bags shooting us questioning glances, I felt like I belonged.

When dessert arrived I dug in with fervor. I'd be hitting the gym first thing the next morning, but it would be worth every miserable second of thigh burning torture for just a mouthful of the decadent dessert I had ordered.

"That looks good," Shane said, staring down at my chocolate mousse. "Can I have a bite?"

I glanced over at his dish of some kind of torte. "Only if I can have a bite of yours."

He grinned. "Okay." He lifted a spoonful of the cake that was filled with whipped cream, nuts, and some kind of jam. "At the same time," he suggested, and I lifted a spoonful of my moose.

It was a very intimate thing to do, feeding each other dessert like we were. I was glad that Cecil had excused himself to take a call from work. My body felt like it was afire as I watched Shane's mouth open and his lips close around the spoon. I felt a little dizzy and wasn't paying attention as he put his own spoon to my lips.

Belatedly, I opened my mouth to accept the bite, but some of the whipped cream smeared at the corner. I licked it away and heard Shane mutter a groan filled curse. "Dammit, Harper. I can't sit here and watch you do things like that without hurting."

I chewed and swallowed my mouthful of torte, giving myself time to figure out how I wanted to respond to his confession. "I'm sorry," was the only response my overheated brain could come up with, however.

"I'm going to kiss you goodnight tonight," he threatened, leaning toward me. "And you are going to kiss me back."

I couldn't have responded if I wanted to. My brain wasn't cooperating enough to think of what to say.

Luckily, Cecil came back from taking care of his business call. Unfortunately, he had to say goodnight. A situation that required his attention had come up and he had to fly to London on the redeye. "Sorry to cut the night short, baby cakes." He kissed my temple. "I'll call you in a few days, okay?"

"Be careful. Don't work too hard." I hugged him close for a moment, always hating to tell him goodbye when I knew he was going to be gone for a while. "Love you, C.C."

He chuckled at the old nickname I had given him when I was a little girl. "Love you more, Harpie." I frowned at his revenge nickname for me. "Take care of my girl, Shane," Cecil said, shaking the rocker's hand.

"I will, sir," Shane promised with sincerity. "Have a safe trip."

Shane

I now knew what other guys were talking about when they said it was a nightmare meeting a girl's parents for the first time. I had been nearly shaking in my sneakers when Harper introduced me to her stepdad.

He was a cool guy and we hit it off. Of course it helped that I had let the man win then filled his belly with expensive steak and even pricier bourbon. I liked Cecil Calloway, and he got top scores for treating Harper so gently.

But I was more than happy to shake his hand goodbye after dinner. I was ready for some quiet time with Harper. I ached to taste her lips again, and that ache was only growing more painful as the evening proceeded. Dessert had been pure torture!

With the bill and generous tip taken care of, I took my girl's hand and we headed out. We were almost out the door when I noticed someone sitting at a corner table with some model that was making a name for herself lately. When he spotted me he raised his hand and waved me over.

Knowing I had to speak to the guy, I tugged Harper toward the couple.

"I thought you were ready to go?"

"I have to say hello to someone." I gave her fingers a gentle squeeze. "Then I'm taking you home and kissing you."

I thought I felt her shiver, and my dick twitched against the fly of my dress pants. I pulled her closer as we reached the other table, trying to disguise my instant reaction to the beautiful creature that had me in her snare, as well as to protect her from the man I was about to introduce her to.

"Stevenson!" Rich Branson greeted us with his megawatt smile. He really needed to stop going to the dentist so much to get his teeth whitened. "How has New York been treating you, man?"

I shook his hand. Technically, Rich was Demon's Wings manager but Emmie was the one that handled all our tour dates and everything else. Since Axton had dropped OtherWorld's contract in the spring, Demon's Wings was Rich's biggest client. Emmie worked her ass off to take care of us, while Rich sat back and played with all the money we brought in for him. The guys and I had been talking about dropping our contract at the end of the year when it came up for renewal.

"It's been good," I told the man honestly. "Drake seems to like his new gig."

"Good, good." Rich hadn't been all that enthusiastic about Drake signing on with *America's Rocker*, but he had little say in what we did in our down time. Of course with Emmie's pregnancy and Nik not wanting to take on big commitments for long tours, free time had been in abundance lately. Which meant Rich wasn't raking in the money off us like he had gotten so used to over the last ten years.

The model sitting at the table cleared her throat, making it sound delicate. I turned my gaze in her direction and nearly rolled my eyes at the way she was sizing me up. Knowing that she wanted my attention, I ignored her and introduced Harper instead. "This is my girl, Harper. Beautiful, this is Rich Branson. He manages the band."

"Hello, Mr. Branson." She offered her hand and I gritted my teeth as Rich latched on.

"What's a nice girl like you doing with Stevenson?" Rich laughed, trying to tug Harper closer. "You should dump him and come talk to me."

Harper pulled her hand free. "I'd rather cut your throat and watch you bleed." Her sweet tone mixed with her feisty words made me hard as a rock. I pulled her back against my chest. Unable to mask my amusement the way I did my sudden raging erection, I laughed.

"Ah, another one," Rich murmured, reaching for his scotch, not at all amused by the rejection.

"Another one?" Harper raised a brow at him.

"Emmie, Layla, Lana." Rich shrugged his thin shoulders. "Beautiful on the outside, pure bitch on the inside."

I tensed, ready to rip the guy's head off for daring to call my girl a bitch when Harper laughed. "You think I'm beautiful?"

Sighing, I pulled her back a few steps. "Baby, you really need to look in the mirror," I whispered against her ear before stepping in front of her.

Rich obviously thought he could speak to my girl any which way. Not only had he insulted her, but also the other women in my family, and I wasn't about to walk away without correcting him. With Harper safely behind me, I bent over the table so I could meet Rich eye-to-eye.

"Speak like that to her, or any other female in my family, and I promise you will live to regret it. How will you afford those little blue pills that keep your dick hard while you fuck fake hos like her if the Demons suddenly drop you on your ass?"

I took pleasure in watching the man pale before straightening. With my hand to the small of Harper's back, I guided her out of the restaurant and into the back of a taxi that had just let a couple out.

"I'm sorry about that." I was quick to apologize to her. "I should never have put you in that position..." I broke off when she started shaking her head.

"It's okay. I'm fine. You are the one I was worried about. Do you normally shake like that when you're upset? Do you have high blood pressure or something?" Her tone was full of concern.

I hadn't even realized I was shaking. I didn't normally let my emotions get the better of me, but my rage at the other man was barely restrained. I wanted to beat the fuck out of him—badly. No one talked about Harper like that! No one.

A gentle hand covered my heart, and just like that I felt the anger start to drain away. Glancing down at her hand on my chest, I felt something deep inside constrict. It was almost painful and totally scary. Without thinking about it, I pressed her into the corner of the taxi's backseat and kissed her.

She had the sweetest taste. My tongue stabbed inside her willing mouth and I sipped her nectar greedily. I wanted more, ached to hold her naked body against my own. I needed to be inside of her; my body was screaming for it—my dick weeping for it.

Instead, I only took what I knew she was ready to give. Each second the kiss lasted I savored, loving how she innocently kissed me back. I was her first kiss, and I was determined to be her last.

Harper

How long the taxi had been sitting in front of my apartment building I wasn't exactly sure. But with the meter running, the taxi driver wasn't exactly complaining about the delay.

With a tortured groan Shane raised his face from my neck, having buried it there several minutes before. His lips had left a scalding trail from my lips to my jaw and down to the base of my neck as he had kissed me. "I don't want you to go," he whispered, kissing my lips quick and hard. "But I know you have to."

My brain was foggy with desire, so I didn't understand. "Why do I have to go?" I whispered back.

Another kiss to the corner of my mouth. "Because you aren't ready. You don't trust me enough."

"But…"

His lips stopped me from saying anything else. My fingers tangled in his hair, and I held on tight, trying to keep up with his demanding kiss. His hands stroked up and down my sides, his thumbs caressing the underside of my breasts, making me dizzy and aching in a way I wasn't sure I had ever felt before.

There was a tap on the window behind Shane, and his head jerked around to see some guy in a suit standing outside on the sidewalk. Muttering a curse, he tossed a bunch of bills at the driver and opened the door. The business man, who I was sure lived on the eleventh floor in my building, was grinning when Shane helped me from the back of the car.

Shane growled something under his breath at the man, who smartly remained quiet before getting into the waiting taxi.

With a hand on the small of my back, Shane guided me inside and pressed the button to call for the elevator. The doorman gave us a nod in greeting but otherwise remained quiet until the elevator's doors were closed behind us.

Shivering with suppressed desire, I leaned against the big man who wrapped his strong arms around me. The trip up to the twelfth floor felt like it took an eternity, yet was over far too soon. His arms tightened for a moment, his lips lingering at my ear, before he finally released me and walked me down the corridor to the corner apartment.

I tried to find the words to ask him to come in. "Do you..."

He shook his head. "No, beautiful. As badly as I want to, I can't come in." He lowered his head and brushed a tender kiss over my lips, then my nose, and lastly over my eyes. It was so sweet that I felt my throat clog with tears. "Can I see you tomorrow?"

All I could do was nod as he stepped back. Our hands were still linked as he started to turn away, holding fast until we could no longer stay linked. "Good night, beautiful," I heard him say as I watched him walk backwards toward the elevators.

I bit my lip and watched until he disappeared behind the elevator doors before opening the front door of my apartment.

Of course no one was home, and I hadn't been expecting them to be. It was Saturday night. Linc was probably on the prowl for a sleepover friend and he must have taken Dallas with him. Just as he was her guard, she was his. As for Lana, I was happy that she was spending yet another night with her Drake.

But that meant I was all alone in our big apartment, with an aching body and a whirling mind. I wanted to talk, take a long cool shower, and fall into bed. Sighing, I locked the door and headed toward my room. A cool shower would have to do.

I was stripping when my phone chimed with Shane's designated text tone. Glancing down at the screen, I saw his message.

<3 <3 <3 I miss u already <3 <3 <3

A goofy smile spread across my face, and I sat down on the edge of my bed, holding my phone close like a love sick fool. Finally, I texted him back.

Wish you had stayed.

Almost instantly he sent a return text. **Me 2. C U tomorrow, beautiful.**

I was determined that I wasn't going to let the attraction I felt for Shane get in the way. We were friends and I wanted it to stay that way.

Each morning I woke with that determination firmly in mind. And it worked until we were alone. His drugging kisses would always bend my resolve, and I would melt against him every time his lips touched mine. It was scary, crazy… Wonderful.

I was developing stronger feelings for the rocker with each passing day. My heart actually ached when he wasn't around, and that was kind of terrifying. Over the last five weeks, I had spent the majority of my free time with Shane. Of course with more and more freelance opportunities coming in, I didn't have as much free time as I was used to.

Work was booming and a few magazines had even mentioned keeping me in mind when they had a position open up. It was exciting and what I'd been dreaming of since I was fifteen, but it couldn't compete with the excitement I felt when I was with Shane.

Today we were at The Ink Shop watching Lana's back transform into a work of art. I was there for moral support, keeping her entertained so her mind wasn't on the needle pressed against sensitive skin. With Dallas, Link, and Shane there to add some variety and humor to the event, Lana was spending more time laughing than thinking about what was going on behind her.

Lana was addicted to ink, just as Dallas was. While I had a tattoo of my own, I hadn't felt that rush of adrenaline like my friends had, and I didn't care if I ever got another one.

The Ink Shop was the place to go if you wanted a great tattoo. Dallas didn't let anyone but the owner work on her. Shane even had one on his right bicep that he'd had done a few years before by the guy that was working on Lana at the moment. Tyler was very professional and handled the tattoo gun with confidence.

"I might get another one soon," Shane said as he fingered through the photo album of past work Tyler had done.

"Yeah?" I glanced at his arms. Most of his ink consisted of skulls, but there were some variations here and there. A star on his left elbow. A black rose on his forearm. I liked them all and had spent hours just tracing them with my finger nails. "What do you have in mind?"

His smile was sly, a little mysterious, and I wondered what was going through his head. "You'll have to wait and see, beautiful."

I rolled my eyes at him.

"Almost done," Tyler assured Lana who was making pained faces. She had been lying face down on the table for nearly four hours now and her back had to be killing her.

"I'm going to catch hell when Emmie show's Jesse and Layla my credit card bill next month," Lana said to no one in particular. "But it will be worth it."

"I could have taken care of it, sis," Shane reminded her, but of course Lana had wanted to pay for it herself, which technically meant that her brother-in-law was paying for her ink.

Lana started to say something, but it turned into a grunt as Tyler went over a particularly sensitive area on her lower back. "Never mind."

"Five more minutes, sweetheart."

It was twenty minutes later before we were heading out the door. Lana had seen the masterpiece on her back, but now it was bandaged up. As we left and walked toward the restaurant where we had decided to have dinner, she kept glancing down at her phone.

I knew she wanted to call Drake, but Shane had talked her into giving it a day before she let him see what she'd done. I thought the angel wings on her back were beautiful, but maybe a little extreme if it was just to tell the guy she loved him. Really, if she loved him why couldn't she just say it and that would be that? Did she have to mark her body to prove it?

But it was her body and she could do whatever she wanted with it.

After dinner the five of us split up. Lana went back to the apartment to crash, while Dallas and Linc were heading to one of their usual clubs. Shane had tempted me with a movie, and I wanted some alone time with him. I was ready to admit that I wanted more than friendship.

I was ready for whatever he thought I still needed time for.

Shane

I was one big ache.

Five weeks of nothing but kissing Harper and I was sure that my balls were going to rupture. I had never gone without, had always taken what was offered. And when we were alone, she was more than willing.

But I had to be sure that she was ready before I took her to the next step. I wanted her to know that no matter what she could trust me with her body—and her heart.

After spending the entire afternoon watching Lana get her back inked with Dallas and Linc, then suffering through dinner, I finally had her alone in the back of a dark theater. The arm rest was up so she could snuggle closer, and I was more interested in how good she felt against me than the movie playing on the screen.

"Do you wear perfume?" I whispered, wondering what scent it was that she wore that drove me out of my mind.

"No, why?"

I nuzzled my nose against her hair. "You smell so good, beautiful. Like lavender and something else."

"Oh, that's just my soap."

Just soap? Fuck, I was jealous of that soap! It got to touch her every day in places I had been slowly dying to take advantage of. Muttering a curse under my breath, I tried to move my dick into a more bearable position. It was hopeless, of course. As hard as I was, there was no position that was bearable.

Harper raised her head. "You okay?"

"No, baby. I'm not okay." My hand rubbed over the painful rod that was resting against my thigh in my jeans. Instead of easing some of my pain, it only added to it. "I'm about two strokes away from coming in my jeans."

She glanced around. We were in the very back of the theater and this was a crap movie, so there weren't many people watching it anyway. Seeing that we were practically all alone, she bit her lip. I nearly cried out when her slender fingers skimmed over my aching dick.

I felt the pre-cum leak onto my thigh. My balls were tight and I was so close. Fuck, I had been this way for over five weeks! Cold showers didn't help any more, and I had never been able to get myself off. It always made me think of that horrible time when I was a kid and Rusty would do things...

"Shane..." Harper breathed my name, her hand exploring the shape of my cock through my jeans. "Take me home with you, Shane."

She didn't have to ask me twice. Grasping her hand, I pulled her up and out of the theater. In less than two minutes, I had her in the back of a taxi headed toward my apartment. I was trembling like an untried teenager. I couldn't keep my legs still as I tried to keep from devouring her in the back seat of a New York cab while the driver watched.

I wasn't against public sex. I'd done it more than a few times at some really insane parties. But that wasn't going to happen with Harper. She deserved more respect than that...unless she wanted it. If my girl wanted public sex, I would give it to her. Anything she wanted.

I doubted, however, that she wanted it tonight.

"Shane?"

Her sweet voice made me turn my head. I had the entire length of the backseat between us so I wouldn't do the things that kept flashing through my head. Such naughty things that involved my beautiful girl, like spreading her wide and eating her pussy, or fingering her until she squirted and soaked the backseat with her intoxicating scent.

"Are you okay?"

I could only nod. I couldn't find my voice. The way I was acting was probably freaking her out. I kept tapping my feet and rocked back and forth to ease some of my pain. My hands were shaking, and I had a cold sweat beading my brow. I probably looked like a crack addict. Shit I was sure that I looked like one.

"Are you in pain?"

"You have no idea." My voice was raspy, full of repressed desire. "Need you so bad."

I couldn't see her eyes and had no clue what she was thinking, but the small smile I saw tilting her lips kept any panic I might have over scaring her at bay.

When the taxi pulled to a stop in front of my building, I tossed a hundred dollar bill at the driver, knowing that the ride hadn't even came close to costing that much. The man thanked me, but I didn't pay attention to him as I pulled Harper out on my side and rushed her toward the entrance.

"Evening, Mr. Stevenson." Kyle, the night doorman, greeted.

I nodded my head at him, punching the call button for the elevators. "Hey, Kyle. My brother home?" It wouldn't matter if he was or not. It would take a natural disaster to stop what was going to happen with Harper.

"About an hour or so ago..."

"Great. Thanks." The elevator doors opened and I pulled Harper in with me.

I wanted to kiss her so fucking bad but knew that if I did, the elevator wasn't going to make it to my apartment before I was between her legs in some shape or form. So I tried to remember every word to the National Anthem. I never could remember the whole thing!

When the elevator stopped on my floor, I practically sprinted down the corridor to my door. Behind me Harper was giggling, so I figured she wasn't too scared of the sex addict about to ravage her.

Harper

If I had known that he was hurting, I would have done something to help him. Now he was half crazy with need, and I found that I was liking every minute of it.

Shane didn't let go of my hand as he unlocked the door of his apartment. When the deadbolt became tricky, he growled something I couldn't understand and banged his fist on the thick door before trying again. My heart was racing with excitement as he swung me off my feet and carried me into the apartment, using his foot to slam the door shut as he practically ran toward his bedroom.

His lips were on my neck before we even reached his bed. I thrust my fingers in his hair and held on tight, sighing with pleasure as he licked and nibbled his way to my ear. "Want you so fucking bad, baby."

Good Lord, I loved how throaty his voice got when he was kissing me. I likened him to an actual demon when it got so deep and raspy like it was now. It made me shiver and gooseflesh pop up along my entire body. My nipples hardened at the sound of that sexy voice, and I ached for him to touch them.

"I want you too," I whispered.

His hands were busy stripping me faster than I could think. My knee length cashmere skirt went flying, followed by the matching shirt. I didn't even try to cover myself as he unfastened my bra and bared my breasts. Even though they were so small, he had told me more than once that he loved my breasts.

"Your tits are so beautiful, baby." He lowered his head and captured one of my nipples while his fingers started tugging on my panties. "You taste as good as you smell!"

Unable to think, there was just too much going on at once, I gave myself over to his experienced hands. I knew that he would take care of me. Something deep inside assured me that Shane would never hurt me when it came to this.

His hands were everywhere: cupping my breasts, pinching my nipples, in my hair, caressing my outer thighs. My need grew with every touch, set my skin aflame in a way that I was sure would leave me with third degree burns before it was all over.

I felt the cool air against my naked flesh before I realized that he had left me. I opened my eyes, looking for him in the darkness. "Sh-Shane?"

"I…I…" I heard his voice along with his labored breathing. "I need a minute, baby. Never been this worked up before."

My heart melted. He could have taken me then and there. Sought out his pleasure and to hell with my own. But he hadn't. Instead, he was trying to make this good for me. I scooted to the end of the bed where he was standing, facing away from me while he tried to get his breathing under control.

When my hand touched his bare back, he tensed but didn't pull away. "Turn around, Shane."

Slowly, he did as I asked. His erection was straining against his jeans. My mouth went dry at how big he looked through the denim material. With trembling fingers, I reached for the top button and released it. Ever so carefully, I lowered the fly, scared that I would hurt him.

My heart felt like it was going to beat me to death as I tugged until his jeans landed at his feet. His hands were balled into tight fists at his sides, his knuckles white. Shane was holding on to his control by a thread and I only wanted to help him.

Linc went around the apartment regularly with nothing on, and I had to admit that I wasn't shy about looking my fill when he did it. But my gay friend had nothing on Shane. Sweet Lord, his dick was pure perfection—long and thick, pink with bright blue veins that pulsed with each of his heartbeats. The head was slick with his pre-cum.

"I'm scared," he whispered.

"Of what?" Shouldn't I be the one scared? I was the virgin.

I watched as he swallowed hard and fell to his knees in front of me. He looked so lost, so tortured, and it made my heart ache for him. Strong arms wrapped around my waist, his head pillowed in my lap. "I want you so bad, but I'm scared that you aren't ready for this. If I rush you, I might lose you."

It was then that I realized that I was already half in love with the rocker. His words broke through some of those stone walls I held erect around my heart, and it was more than a little terrifying to feel them crumbling. But I liked it and wanted to see where this thing with us could lead.

Combing my fingers through his hair, I lowered my head and kissed his cheek. "Come lie with me, Shane," I murmured. "I want you to hold me."

Slowly, he lifted his head. I scooted back until I found the pillows and lay down before lifting a hand toward him. He climbed in beside me, and I waited until he was comfortable before pillowing my head on his shoulder. "Baby?"

I smiled as I turned my face into his chest and kissed a spot right over his heart. "Don't be scared, okay?" Raising my head, I met his blue-gray gaze.

"I'm sorry…" he began, but I shook my head and he shut up.

"Shh. Don't speak." I lifted myself up onto my elbow and let my free hand trail across his chest. His heart was still beating fast.

Shane was quiet as I let my hand wander. My fingers traced over his abs. They were hard and ridged. His skin was hot and smooth, and I wondered if it was naturally like that or if he shaved it. I stopped at his naval and let my index finger slip inside to explore. He groaned and shivered, and I glanced up for a quick peek at his face.

His face was one of masculine perfection. Strong and bold. I loved the curve of his jaw. His nose fascinated me because I had never thought of that particular facial feature as sexy before, but on him it was. His eyes were darker, like a stormy sea. And his mouth...

I wanted his wicked mouth on every part of my body.

But not yet. Not until I gave him what he needed.

"Tell me if I'm doing it wrong," I commanded as I let my hand skim down his stomach. When I reached the base of his erection, I hesitated for only a second before wrapping my fingers around his girth.

"Fuck! Harper..."

I tightened my hold on him and stroked upward until I felt the liquid heat of his pre-cum at the head. He grew longer and thicker in my hand, and I stroked downward until I found his balls. I watched like a voyeur as each stroke produced more and more of the intoxicating scented liquid at the tip and used my thumb to spread it.

Shane started to pant and I increased my speed, stroking harder and faster. His fingers tangled in my hair, and I couldn't help but feel proud that I was making him feel so good.

"Baby, I'm close. So close."

Curious about the taste of the sweet smelling liquid his dick kept producing, I stopped stroking and he let out a whimper. "Please, don't stop," he groaned.

I ignored his plea. Bending forward, I took the tip into my mouth, licking away the thick, clear liquid. I didn't know if I liked the taste or not, so I licked it again. Moaning when the taste exploded on my tongue, I licked him harder, taking more of him into my mouth. He grew even harder, stretching my mouth as far as it could go.

"Harper, I'm going to come in your mouth," he growled.

His words thrilled me and I sucked the tip harder, my teeth accidently nipping him a time or two. Both of my hands encircled his shaft and stroked him while I continued to suck and lick the head. His hands clenched in the bed covers on each side of him, his breathing growing more ragged as I took him just a little deeper and he hit the back of my throat.

"Oh. Fuck!" he shouted, his back arching as he thrust deep into my mouth and I felt the first salty spray of his climax.

Had I died?

I was sure that if I hadn't died I was hanging in some kind of limbo, one where your entire body felt like it was floating away. My mind was blank, my body numb. I wasn't even sure I was breathing.

I could honestly tell you that more than a thousand girls had sucked my dick in my lifetime. Some had really known what they were doing, while others had looked at it as just something to do to get the rock star off.

And then there was Harper.

She had been clumsy and completely inexperienced. She had left her teeth marks from where she had accidentally bitten me more than once. But nothing could compare to how good she made me feel, how crazy I'd been as I sought out my release in her hot little mouth.

Now, as I slowly floated back down from the biggest climax of my fucking life, I found that I was still struggling to catch my breath. Her head was lying on my stomach while she trailed her nails up and down my still half-hard cock. "Baby?"

Caramel hair shifted over my abdomen as she turned her head, and I was assaulted by those gorgeous violet eyes. I could see the pent up desire burning deep in their depths, but what had me catching my breath was the one look I had hoped to see there since I realized just how I felt for her.

Maybe she didn't even realize it yet, but I knew that she cared just as deeply as I did.

"Still scared?" she murmured, tracing her nails up and down the length of my stiff shaft.

Reaching out, I cupped her beautiful face. "Terrified," I assured her with complete sincerity.

I flipped Harper onto her back. We fit just as I knew we would—perfectly. The way she spread her legs for me, so trusting. My cock fit like a missing puzzle piece against her. The way those incredible breasts pushed against my chest. She was my other half, and I was going to show her just how perfect we were for each other.

I wanted to tell her. The need to make promises that I intended to keep to my last breath was almost overwhelming. I knew she wasn't ready to hear them. So I showed her instead.

I could taste myself on her lips when I kissed her. It wasn't a great taste, and it brought back so many horrible memories. I tensed and started to draw back, but the gentle touch of her hands on my back soothed me. I left her mouth, kissing down her throat and across her collar bone.

She made a small little mewling sound as I took her nipple into my mouth, her lower body arching and rubbing against my cock almost unconsciously. My girl's tits were super sensitive. I sucked harder, switching from one nipple to the other every few moments. Her fingers scraped across my scalp, holding me to her.

"Shane…"

My hand skimmed down her side and over her mound. Knowing that she was hurting and that I was the only one that could ease the pain, I spread the outer lips of her drenched pussy.

"Sh-shane!" she whimpered my name as my thumb teased across her clit.

"Do you like this?" I wanted to know everything she did and didn't like, only ever wanted to give her mind numbing pleasure.

"Y-yes."

I pressed my thumb a little harder, rubbing in little circles while I watched her eyes for signs of pleasure or pain. "This?" I felt her liquid desire flowing, dampening her thighs before she could even nod. My fingers trailed lower, diving into her wet depths.

She was so tight! I knew she was a virgin, and I had had my share of them as a teenager. But I couldn't remember any of them ever being this tight. Her heat scalded me, making my dick ache like it had not just come the hardest it had ever come before.

"Don't you play with this pretty pussy, baby?"

Harper shook her head. "No."

"Ever?"

"No." She bit her lip. "I've never wanted to. No one has ever even made me want this but you."

If it had been anyone but Harper saying that, I probably would have run for the fucking hills. Instead, I was filled with proud arrogance. "No one else ever will, beautiful."

She flinched and I was worried that I had hurt her. "Baby?"

"Say it again," she whispered.

I frowned. "Say what, baby?"

"Call me beautiful. When you say it, I almost believe you."

My jaw clenched. It wasn't the first time that she had said something stupid along those lines. I wanted to rip apart whoever had made her believe that she wasn't beautiful.

"Baby, you are so beautiful you make my chest ache just looking at you." I brushed a kiss over her forehead. "I have never seen anything—ever—that compares to the beauty I see before me right now."

"Shane…"

I kissed her lips quick and hard to shut her up, not wanting to hear her argue. "Tomorrow you are going to tell me who put such crazy nonsense in that pretty head of yours. But tonight, you are going to lie back and let me prove just how beautiful I know you are."

Harper

The first brush of his lips over my clit made all thoughts evaporate.

Maybe I should have felt self-conscious, but I didn't. How could I possibly feel like that with Shane? For once in my life I really did feel beautiful.

His tongue teased over my folds, dipping inside. It was so good. That little brush of his tongue inside of me was so intense my fingers fisted in the covers beneath me. I was powerless to stop the sounds that escaped me.

Callused hands cupped my breasts, pinching my nipples and twisting gently. It made muscles deep inside clench, and I felt my sex flooding with hot desire. This was all new territory for me. I had never touched myself, never had an orgasm. Shane had awakened the woman in me.

He sucked my clit into his mouth, making me cry out his name as he let go with a little *pop* before sucking it again. Over and over again, he tortured me with that sweet pleasure while one of his fingers tenderly thrust into me, stopping short of the barrier that was proof of my virginity.

"You taste so fucking good, beautiful," Shane told me between sucks. "Does this feel good?"

"Yes!" I cried. "So, so good!"

He stiffened his tongue, skimming over my clit in a barely there caress that had me begging for more. He added another finger, thrusting just a little harder as my body became accustomed to his gentle invasion. I could feel something quickening inside of me as my entire body felt like it had caught fire.

"That's it, baby. Let go," his throaty voice commanded.

"Wh-what about you?" I asked, panting hard. I could feel him pulsing. I didn't want him hurting like he had been earlier.

"Do you want my dick, baby?" He lifted his head just enough to meet my gaze. "I don't want to rush you into something that you aren't ready for..."

I was ready for anything he was willing to give me, and I told him so. Shane grinned. "Oh, the possibilities, sweet Harper." He lifted onto his knees and spread my thighs even wider.

I thought for sure he was going to take me, fill me, and make the empty feeling deep inside go away. Instead, he gripped his beautiful cock in his hand and rubbed the tip over my clit. My hands found his thighs and I sunk my nails deep into his flesh. That brush of his dick across sensitive tissue was so perfect. "I like that."

"Me too." He did it again, his free hand spreading my outer lips wide while he rubbed against me harder.

He felt like silk covered stone. His heat added fuel to my already raging inferno. His hips started to thrust gently, his dick slipping just a little lower with each caress up and down my slick folds. When the head teased at my entrance, my inner walls clenched in anticipation, but he only went back to rubbing my clit.

"Shane, I need you!" I whimpered, arching my hips in invitation to take me.

"I can't stop," he growled. "Don't ask me to stop."

"I want you inside me."

"I can't." His jaw clenched in an attempt to hold back. "Condoms are too far away. I'm going to come..."

"Please…" It was so intense, and I could feel my orgasm building, building, building! But I needed him to fill me, needed him deep inside of me as I came around his hard cock.

"Baby!" Shane groaned my name, the tip of his dick slipping inside of me.

I couldn't hold back the scream as my body came apart. He wasn't even completely in me, but it was all I needed. My muscles began to spasm, clenching around the head of his dick. He growled something, but I was too far gone to understand.

I didn't feel him pull out and was lost in my own paradise of sensations as he covered my stomach with his thick release.

How long it took me to recover I wasn't sure. Days, hours, minutes. But when I did Shane was there, his arms holding me close. His lips brushed over my temple. "Sleep, beautiful. There's no way in hell you are leaving my bed tonight."

Shane

I'm not sure what had made me get up.

There I was, half-asleep with Harper's sweet rear pressed against my semi-hard cock. She was sleeping peacefully, her hair over my arm and pillow in a way I would remember for the rest of my life. The sight of this girl, the only one that would ever hold my heart so tightly, lying in my bed was just too perfect. How had I gone so long without this, without *her*?

But there was this anxious feeling in the pit of my stomach that was telling me to get up and go check on Drake.

When it started to really hurt, I carefully untangled myself from Harper and glanced at the clock. Just after one o'clock. Frowning, I pulled on a pair of boxers that I only wore when I was working out or when I was too lazy to put clothes on around the house. Quietly, so as not to disturb the sleeping beauty snuggled in my bed, I left the room and went down the hall to my brother's room.

That all too familiar scent of sweat and hard liquor hit me as soon as I turned the knob and cracked the door open an inch or so. Dread hit the bottom of my stomach like a lead weight.

"No, Drake," I muttered to myself.

He had called me earlier that day, and I should have stopped and thought for a minute before brushing it off as nothing. He was probably calling to tell me he was having cravings, that he needed me to take him to a meeting. Feeling guilty, I pushed the door open a little more and stepped inside.

All that guilt evaporated when I saw the girl lying on the bed with my brother and was replaced with white hot rage.

"Fuck!" I practically yelled, but the two sleeping forms on the bed didn't even move. "Drake, what the fuck did you do?"

The next few hours were hard ones to get through, most of which I spent on my own except for the brief visit by Lana. I felt gutted after watching her walk away with that dead expression in her pretty amber eyes. With Emmie on her way—along with Jesse and Layla—there wasn't much I could do but pace.

I could have woken Harper up and asked her to be with me through the long wait, but I didn't want to upset her.

It was after nine before Emmie unlocked the front door, and she and Layla walked into the apartment, followed by a brooding Jesse. Perhaps I should have felt sorry for my brother, but I was still too angry to care right then.

Seeing Emmie was like a balm to my heart. I pulled her into a tight bear hug, holding her close for the first time in what felt like a lifetime but was only a couple of months. "Thanks for coming."

She sighed. "I don't know how much good I can do."

"How is Lana?" Layla demanded, her face pale and her eyes blood shot.

"I don't know, Layla," I told her honestly. "She was so calm, so unlike herself. Lana doesn't do calm when slapped in the face."

"No, she runs all the way across the country," Jesse bit out, his hands clenched at his sides. "All the good it did, too. Wake his fucking ass up, Shane!"

"I've tried. He's out cold. Drake hasn't had anything harder than coffee in months. Whatever he got into last night hit him hard.

We just have to let him sleep it off." Then I was sure that I would be picking my brother up off the floor.

I made sure my three guests were comfortable before I returned to my bedroom to wake Harper. She was still sleeping peacefully. I took a moment to look down at her spread across my sheets. One hand was tucked under her cheek, the other across her stomach, that mouth with the perfect Cupid's bow parted as she lightly snored every other breath.

I climbed in behind her, letting her warmth chase away the coldness that had invaded my body the moment I found my brother asleep in the same bed as Gabriella Moreitti. As soon as I touched her, I felt calmer and ready to face the disaster that Drake had created for himself, and therefore all of us.

She mumbled something in her sleep before blinking her eyes open. "Shane?"

I kissed her shoulder. "Good morning, sleeping beauty."

Her yawn was adorable and I waited until she cuddled into my chest before I told her what had been happening while she slept. The more I said the tenser she became. Worried for her friend, she started to get up. "I have to get home. She must be devastated."

"I'll take you," I promised, not bothering to avert my eyes as I watched her dress. Her breasts swayed ever so slightly with each movement she made.

"But you have guests."

"They aren't here to see me, Harper. In fact, I'm sure it will make them all calmer if I'm not around right now. All I do is pace and that can get irritating after a while." And Emmie was in no mood to be irritated. I would rather face the flames of Hell than get on her bad side.

When she was finally dressed she pulled her hair into a sloppy bun at the back of her neck and turned to face me. "I wasn't exactly planning on meeting your family this soon."

"Are you nervous?"

A small smile tilted her lips. "Were you nervous when I introduced you to Cecil?" I made a sour face and she laughed. "Then you have your answer."

"There is no need to be nervous of Emmie and Layla. And especially not Jesse. They will love you, baby." *Just as I do...*

I kissed her lips and lead her out into the living room.

From the moment I realized I had feelings for Harper, I had told Emmie all about her. She wasn't surprised when I introduced her to the girl that had captured my heart. Emmie tried to be nice, but she had too much going through her mind to pay much attention to Harper. Layla and Jesse shook her hand, and even welcomed her to the family, but were otherwise stone faced.

As soon as I could, I took Harper home. I didn't want Harper around the tension and would hate it if she thought that my family didn't like her.

My girl was right by my side over the next few days. I had to be there for my brother, but Harper was always there for *me* when I needed her. She was strong, stronger than even I had realized. When everyone else was stressed to the max, she was the calm one. Even Emmie took notice of it and took me aside to let me know that she really liked Harper.

"She's really sweet, Shane."

We were standing by the double doors that went to the ICU where Lana had been for the last three days. Behind Emmie was the waiting room where we'd all been camped out since Lana's emergency surgery to stop the bleeding from her complicated miscarriage. I could see Harper sitting with Layla and Lucy, who'd arrived with Nik and Mia two days ago.

Lucy was still looking upset, worried about her sister. But Harper was talking softly to her and stroking Lucy's short hair back from her face.

"I know." I was turned toward Harper, ready to go to her in an instant if she needed me.

She grasped my hand, bringing my focus back to her. "She's really good for you. Even through all this craziness I can see that." Emmie sighed and shook her head. "I've really put my foot in it with Lana. I'm not even sure why I put all the blame on her. You know I love her. She's Drake's other half…"

"Emmie, I think it's obvious why you are so hard on her." I leaned back against the wall, trying to get a better glimpse of Harper. Just looking at her calmed my nerves. "Drake has always been the one that needed you most, whether we want to admit it or not. You were acting like a mother bear protecting her cub, and that's great.

But the cub fucked up, sweetheart. And it was no one's fault but his own."

"Yeah, I know."

The lost look in her big green eyes hurt me, and I pulled her close. "It's going to be okay, Em. Lana will be alright, and you can kiss and make up. She knows how you are. She won't hold it against you."

"Don't let me do this to Harper, Shane."

I laughed. "Don't worry. If you say one word that hurts my girl, I'll be all over your ass about it." No way was I letting anyone—not even Emmie—hurt Harper in any way.

Harper

Lana had finally woken up and stayed awake this time.

For three days she was in and out of it, whether it was the meds they were giving her or what, I wasn't sure. But I was so glad that my friend had finally come back to us.

Everyone was exhausted, both physically and especially emotionally. The doctor had come into the OR waiting room right after Lana had gotten out of surgery and explained to us that Lana had come close to dying. If she hadn't gotten to the hospital when she had, she would have bled to death for sure. But there had been no complications during surgery, so she was going to make a full recovery.

With Lana now awake, and able to talk, she wasted little time in demanding everyone go home and get some sleep. Layla and Drake had argued, but Lana being Lana, had gotten her way in the end.

After sleeping in a hard plastic chair for the last few days, I was ready for my bed.

Linc and Dallas were on their way out; unlike me, they hadn't been at the hospital day and night. Dallas hadn't heard about Lana until the day after it had happened, and Linc had been at work. Figuring Shane would want to spend some time with his family, I called my goodbyes and started for the elevators with my roommates.

"Wait!" Shane called just before the doors closed.

Linc hit the *open door* button, forcing the elevator to pause and retract the sliding door. I started to step forward to ask Shane what was wrong when he pushed me back inside and hugged me against his side.

"Are you okay?" I demanded, looking up at his pale face and noticing the dark circles under his eyes.

He hadn't been lying about the pacing thing. He had paced, and paced, and paced some more. Emmie had growled at him to sit down more than a few times. Even during the middle of the night, when we were all trying to catch a nap, he would alternate between pacing and holding me. Where the hell had he gotten the energy to do all that pacing?

"I need to be close to you," he murmured against my ear so only I could hear.

His warm breath against my ear made me shiver, and I wasn't feeling quite as tired as I had been just moments before. Biting my lip, I snuggled deeper into his side, relaxing against him as he played with the ends of my hair and the elevator descended.

Dallas, who was always mouthy, had been noticeably quiet the last few times she had come to visit. Even as good as I was feeling being with Shane, I noticed her troubled expression as we rode home together in the back of a taxi. When we got home I asked Shane to go ahead and shower while I talked to my friend.

As soon as my bedroom door closed behind him, I tackled Dallas. "What's the matter?"

She swallowed hard but didn't answer as she sat down on the couch, reaching for the remote to the television instead. With Linc in the kitchen fixing a quick dinner, I knew that I couldn't count on him for back up. So I stood in front of the flat screen, forcing her to meet my gaze. "I'll stand here for days if I have to, Dallas."

"I don't want to talk about it, Harp." Her jaw was tense, her body vibrating with emotions, but her eyes were glazed with tears.

Dallas wasn't a crier. I don't think I had ever seen her cry.

"Is it about Drake and Lana?" Dallas and Linc had been at the same party as Drake when he had gotten drunk. She had told me that she didn't think he'd slept with Gabriella because she had seen things at the party that suggested that Gabriella had already hooked up with someone before the other girl had taken Drake home.

"No. I swear." She sighed and pulled her legs under her. "Drake wasn't a big fan of Gabriella's, even as drunk as he was."

"Then what's wrong?" I waved my hand at her. "This isn't you, Dallas."

"I think Axton hooked up with Gabriella at the party," she burst out. "One minute he was beside me, the next he was gone. I didn't put it together until I got to the hospital, but when I went looking for Ax he was coming out of one of the bedrooms. A few minutes later, while I was talking to Drake and Linc, I saw her come down the hall looking like she had just gotten the fucking of her life." A tear escaped the corner of her eye. "When I asked Ax about it, he didn't deny it. Just brushed it off…"

The tear broke my heart for her. I fell down on the edge of the couch beside her and hugged her tight. "I'm sorry, sweetie."

Dallas was stiff in my arms, but I wasn't expecting anything different. She really hated to be touched. "He loves her. Her fucking name is on his wrist, for fuck's sake! Of course he wants her. I'm just a distraction…"

I didn't know what to say, so I just sat there holding her while she vented. When she was done she went to her room and slammed the door shut. Sighing, I stood, feeling more drained than I had an hour ago.

Linc stuck his head out of the kitchen door. "Want something to eat?"

I grimaced. "Nah, but thanks. I'm beat. See you in the morning."

"Night. If you need anything just call out."

I offered him a smile before heading toward my room. I was pretty sure it was just my room now. Lana was most likely moving in with Drake. I could hear the shower still going when I shut the door behind me. Shane had left a trail of clothes leading to the bathroom, and I shook my head as I picked up his T-shirt and then his jeans.

Socks were next, and just as I had expected, no underwear. My man didn't seem to like underwear all that much.

I stopped mid-step and a goofy smile lifted my lips. *My man?*

Yeah, he had proved that he was my man over the last few days. Constantly touching me, including me in his unusual family. Even with the crisis going on, it had felt like I belonged with the strange friends that had united as a family. Shane had made sure of it.

"Baby?"

I raised my eyes to find my man sticking his head out of my small shower. His head was soapy and he needed a shave badly. Water glistened off his muscular shoulders and what I could see of his chest. My sex flooded with need.

"Do you need something?" I asked, trying to think about anything but the deliciously sexy, dripping wet man just a few feet away.

"Do you have a razor I can use, beautiful? I don't want to scratch you with this beard."

The thought of that scruff scratching the delicate skin between my thighs while he licked and tongued my sex had me close to whimpering. I clenched my thighs together to ease some of the ache. "Um…No, sorry. I wax." I dropped his clothes on the sink, and reached for my shirt. "Let's keep the beard."

I could actually feel his gaze on me as I continued to strip with my back turned toward him. The air around me felt tense with his arousal, and I felt a sense of power as I took my time showing him my body inch by inch. Just moments before I had felt so tired, but with the promise of more of the pleasure I had experienced Saturday night, my body came alive.

Wet arms wrapped around my waist from behind as a damp, male body pressed against me. He was warm from the hot shower, hard with suppressed arousal. "You are so fucking beautiful, Harper."

For the first time I didn't question if it was true or not. When I was with Shane, I *was* beautiful. I turned in his strong arms, pressing my bare chest to his. With my arms around his neck, I stood tiptoe and softly brushed my lips against his. "Will you make love to me, Shane?"

His eyes darkened and I felt his cock twitch against my stomach. "Let's get you clean first, beautiful." His raspy voice sent delightful shivers down my spine.

Shane's arms tightened around me as he lifted me and placed me in the shower with him. The water felt divine on my slightly sore body. Thanks to my hospital bedside vigil, I'd slept in awkward positions over the last few days. Shane filled his hands with body wash and massaged my body from head to toe with the lavender scented soap.

Callused hands from years of playing guitar caressed over sensitive skin, making my breasts swell and my nipples harden. I held onto the side of the shower as slippery fingers parted the lips of my sex, teasing the bundle of nerves hidden between the folds. My thighs trembled and I couldn't hold back a cry of pleasure as his thumb pressed down just firm enough to give me what I needed.

"I've needed you so bad, baby." His lips trailed down my throat while his fingers slipped inside to play with a wetness that had nothing to do with the shower.

"Me too," I moaned as his middle finger thrust deep, but not deep enough to touch my virginity. "I had a few fantasies of finding an empty hospital room and begging you to use your tongue on me again."

"You should have told me," Shane growled, going back to my lips and kissing what little breath I had from me. "I would have made it a reality."

"There's always next time," I teased.

"Fuck, I don't want to go through that again." He leaned his forehead against mine, breathing hard. "It was scary, and all I could think was it could have just as easily been you..." I felt him shudder and watched in fascination as he swallowed hard. Blue-gray eyes were glassy as they met mine. "I don't know what I would do if I lost you."

My heart turned over, hard. I gasped—half in pain, half in surprise. Shane was so open about his emotions. I could see everything he was feeling shining back at me through those eyes of his, and it both thrilled and terrified me. I pushed the fear down, though, and concentrated on the thrill for now.

"I'm not going anywhere," I promised him, hoping that the feelings I had for him were shining through my own eyes. I didn't have the courage to tell him aloud what I felt for him.

He pulled his fingers from between my thighs, and I whimpered in protest. My rocker only smiled and washed my hair. Firm fingers rubbing my scalp was a new pleasure in and of itself. I groaned as he rinsed my hair and then added conditioner.

When I was clean he turned the water off and stepped out. Before I could follow, he was there with a towel, wrapping it around me and lifting me from the shower. A second towel appeared and he dried my hair carefully before lifting me once more and carrying me into the bedroom.

Most of my body was still damp from the shower, but so was his. As he laid my body across the twin mattress and followed, I found that our damp skin made for an erotic slip and slide. Shane's hands were not idle. They found my breasts, pushing them together and squeezing. I watched in a trance as he licked the first one then the other with the flat of his tongue before sucking my nipple deep into his hot mouth. His tongue pressed the hardened nipple to the roof of his mouth, and the pulling motions from his strong suction made muscles deep inside clench.

He only lingered long enough to make me whimper before he was kissing me again. My lips and then my neck, his teeth nipped at my ear before licking down to the pulse rapidly beating at the base. I wanted him to kiss my breasts again, but he only smiled when I arched my back in a silent plea and rubbed his rough jaw across them as he trailed kisses over my stomach.

His hands parted my thighs as his kisses trailed lower. For a moment his nose hovered over my throbbing clit, but he only breathed deep. "I love the way you smell, baby. So warm and aroused for me. I could live off the taste of you…"

Despite his words, he didn't kiss me there. His lips moved to the inside of my right thigh, and he sucked on the tender flesh while his fingers combed through the damp curls that surrounded my sex. I could feel the blood rushing to the surface where he was sucking and knew that he was leaving his mark. I loved it and wanted him to mark me again and again. It didn't matter that no one else would ever see the love bites he was leaving. I knew they were there and that was enough.

I raised my head, watching while he left the burning little marks. It was exciting to watch his dark head moving between my legs like that. He moved from one thigh to the other, leaving one purple spot after another. I loved the way the rough scruff felt against the inside of my thighs.

"I could do this all night!"

"Please don't." I pushed his hair back from his face so I could meet his gaze. "I need you, Shane."

His head lifted. "I need you too, babe." His lips brushed across my stomach again, following the trail back up to my mouth.

Needing to touch him, I reached between us and grasped his thick cock. His groan of approval made my already erratic heart beat even faster. I wanted to give him pleasure, wanted to make him just as insane with desire as I was. I pushed on his chest at the same time as I rolled from beneath him.

"What are you doing?" he murmured as I pushed him against my pillows.

"Whatever I want." I grinned when he chuckled. "I want to taste you again, Shane."

The chuckle turned into a growl, and I bit my lip as I glanced down at his pulsing dick. *Next time*, I promised myself. Next time, I would trace every vein with my tongue. This time, I simply wanted to drive him close to the edge.

I gripped him with my right hand then lowered my head and ran my tongue over the thick head of his cock. As I stroked upward, a drop of his pre-cum beaded on the tip and I was quick to lick it away. I loved the taste of him!

I was clumsy, my teeth nipping him from time to time as I took him deep into my mouth. I thought I was hurting him, but he only groaned and begged me not to stop. "Best I've ever had!" he ground out. "Love your little mouth!"

I could feel him growing bigger with each passing minute. But I wanted him to come with me, like the last time we had been together.

"Harper!" he cried when I stopped and straddled his waist.

"Tell me you're clean," I commanded. It was the only thing stopping me from taking what I wanted right that instant. I had to make sure he wasn't going to give me something from his years of hard-core sex with random girls.

"Yes. Em makes us all get tested every three months. I just had a complete physical two months ago." His hands gripped my waist, holding on tight. "There hasn't been anyone since I've met you, baby."

"Good." I covered his hands, squeezing his fingers as I told him what I wanted. "I want you inside of me, Shane. I want you to take what I will only be able to give to one man."

"Oh, Gods!" He closed his eyes for a moment, his hands tightening on my hips. "I want that so bad. But I don't have anything…"

I covered his lips with my fingers, stopping his flow of words. "You don't need it. I've been on the pill since I was fourteen." Painful, irregular periods had forced me to start birth-control to help with the problem.

"Are you trying to kill me, beautiful?" He flipped me so fast that I squealed. Chuckling, he kissed my lips quick and hard. "I've never been with a girl without a condom. Never. So this will be a first for me too."

I thought that he would take me then and there, especially when he had been so close just a few moments ago. Instead, he kissed me. His hands cupped both of my breasts as his tongue tangled with mine. I loved kissing Shane and the way he could make that one simple, intimate act seem so soul consuming.

His cock was lying heavily on my stomach, hot and damp from his own liquid desire as it wept for me. I skimmed my fingertips over the thick head, delighting in his shivers.

He broke away from the kiss long enough to say, "Easy, baby. I'm holding on by a thread here. Too much of your soft hands and I won't be any good to you for a good twenty minutes."

Not wanting any length of a delay to stop him from becoming a part of me, I dropped my hands down on either side of me and gripped the sheets to keep from touching him again. Shane grinned and returned to kissing me. His hands stroked up and down my sides, traveling farther and farther with each downward stroke.

When his thumbs reached my pelvic bone, he kept going. Down, down, down until his index finger spread my lips. I bit the inside of my cheek to keep from crying out, remembering that I had roommates that would be sure to critique our love session come morning. His thumb was doing things that were driving me to the edge of madness, and I swallowed my screams with difficulty.

"I don't want to hurt you, beautiful," he breathed against my ear. "I need you to come for me, baby. Need your pretty pussy drenched with your sweet liquid heat so I'll fit just right inside you."

I thought that I hated dirty talk. It had always embarrassed me in the past when my friends would start talking like that, but Shane's dirty mouth only added fuel to the flames licking deep inside of me. Licking my lips, I arched against his talented fingers, rocking my hips in time to his thrusting hand.

His lips left mine, nearly swallowing my breast as he sucked my nipple into his hot mouth. I could feel myself getting closer, closer, so much closer! His thumb pressed down and moved in tight little circles, making me wetter.

My thighs tensed and I threw my head back, unable to hide my pleasure as I cried his name. As I came around his fingers, he thrust deeper, breaking through my barrier. There was an intense burning as he broke my hymen with his fingers, but the pleasure he was giving me took away from the discomfort.

As soon as the barrier was gone, he pulled his fingers away and lifted himself onto his knees. I was still half-lost in the high of coming apart from just his fingers. I got a quick look at how damp his cock was from his pre-cum before he was pushing it inside me. It was a tight fit, like a puzzle piece being forced into place. Before he was halfway inside of me, he was cursing and grinding his teeth.

"You feel like Heaven!" His hands gripped each ass cheek, spreading me wider so he could slide deeper. My walls clung to him like a damp glove. I began to ache, the burn growing worse as he pushed farther, rocking back and forth to ease his passage.

"Shane…" I could only whisper his name, still breathless from my orgasm and the pain that I was starting to feel.

He must have seen something in my eyes that told him I wasn't enjoying this as much as he was. Shane stopped. He held himself completely still inside of me. Licking his thumb, he used it to rub across my clit, making little sparks of pleasure fire through my sex. Soon I was falling apart for him, and he started rocking his hips again.

I could tell he was having a hard time holding back, but he was doing it for me. His jaw was clenched so hard I was sure he'd break some teeth, but he kept his thrusts slow and tender. My emotions rose and choked me. Shane was making my first time so wonderful, so memorable. Even as my inner muscles clenched around his thick length, coming for him again, a tear escaped my eyes.

"Har-per?" He broke my name in half as he raised a trembling hand to wipe away my tear. "Hurting you?"

I shook my head. "No! It's just… This is so beautiful," I whispered.

"Yeah, it is. It is beautiful when two people feel this deeply for each other." He kissed my lips, his hips rocking a little faster now as I sensed his climax building.

I thrust my fingers into his unkempt hair, locking gazes with him as I felt him growing longer, harder, and thicker. Wrapping my legs around his waist to hold him deep inside, I watched in fascination as his eyes turned more gray than blue and he went still above me. That's when I felt it—felt the thick spray of his release, felt his shaft twitching as he came apart deep inside of me.

His eyes rolled back in his head and he fell across me with a shout of my name. "Love you," I thought he muttered against my ear before he went limp.

Chapter Thirteen

Shane

Late summer sunlight peeked through the blinds. Grunting, I snuggled against the warm body resting against my own. When my movements made Harper mumble a protest, I grinned and kissed her shoulder.

"Morning, beautiful."

"Go back to sleep," she commanded. "There is no way I'm getting up this early."

Laughing softly, I glanced at the alarm clock across the room by Lana's bed. It was after ten. "The morning is nearly over, love," I informed her.

She turned over to face me, and my breath caught in my lungs. This was how I always wanted to picture her...No makeup to hide her beauty from me. No glasses or contacts to hinder the natural color of her eyes. Caramel blonde hair spread out around her, tousled from our night of lovemaking. No clothes to hide that glorious body from me.

The small glare she gave me only added to her appeal, and my body was already responding. "If you want to keep your fingers in prime working order, Shane, then you had better shut your sexy mouth and go back to sleep. Or get up. Whichever keeps you quiet long enough for me to go back to sleep for a few more hours."

I flexed my fingers in front of her face, taunting her before using them to tickle her. She screamed then started giggling as I attacked unrelentingly. "Get your beautiful ass up, woman!" I was the one making the demands this time.

"Make me!"

My dick twitched at her provocative words, and I stopped moving. She went completely still when she felt how hard I was against her stomach. Violet eyes turned to indigo and I was lost. "I'm going to love you again, Harper."

Her eyes dilated with the pleasure my words brought her, her little pink tongue coming out to moisten her lips. "O-okay."

"I'll be gentle," I promised, knowing she had to be more than a little sore after the way I had taken her last night. Being gentle hadn't ever been something I excelled at. I liked it rough, fast, and more often than not, hard-core. But for my Harper, I would give her anything and everything she needed.

"I know you will." Her soft reply and the look of complete trust in her beautiful eyes made a lump form in my throat, and I had to clear it a few times before I could breathe again.

Wanting to taste her, I kissed her lips, sucking her readily offered tongue deep into my mouth. I loved how her breasts were just barely a handful, the way her pebble hard nipples rubbed against the palm of my hand. The way she kissed me harder when I pinched those sensitive little nubs drove me mad.

Her legs spread for me without any coaxing. I fit so perfectly against her, my dick sliding between her lips, rubbing her wet little pussy without entering her. She was dripping, her pussy flooding with her arousal more and more with each stroke of my cock moving up and down between her folds. The kiss continued, her moans escaping from time to time as we came up for air, and then we went back to making love with our tongues.

When I knew that I couldn't hold back much longer, I flipped us so that I was lying on my back and she was straddling my thighs.

With trembling hands, she pushed her hair away from her face. I lifted her hips until her sweet pussy was right over the tip of my cock. Her thighs were already trembling, and I swallowed my groan as the head of my dick slipped between those wet folds.

"You can take me as deep as you want like this, baby," I told her, guiding her down just a little more.

She pressed her soft hands to my chest to steady herself and took more of me. I released my hold on her, scared that I would force myself deeper than she could take. With my fists clenched at my sides, I let her have complete control over our lovemaking.

Gods, she was beautiful! The way her hair was tossed back, except for a few strands falling into her eyes. Her body honey kissed with a summer tan. Tits heaving as she panted. Flat stomach quivering with each rock of those glorious hips. And that pussy! The way her lips were spread just enough to let me see her clit and how it flowered in arousal.

Another inch brought her almost halfway down my dick. Her breasts bounced as she lifted and slid back down again. With each downward stroke of her tight pussy, she took more of me. I felt her muscles already tightening around me, letting me know that she was close.

She wasn't the only one. I was barely holding on, ready to blow inside of her at any moment.

When she was finally able to take all of me, I cried out in triumph. "Don't fucking move or I'm going to explode."

"Do it!" she commanded, just as I felt her inner walls begin to spasm around my cock.

She didn't move, didn't have to. Just the feel of those contracting muscles was enough to shoot me to the stars.

After we showered together, I left Harper to dress while I went in search of the coffee I had smelled earlier. I expected one or both of her roommates to be up, but neither were present when I walked into the kitchen in nothing but a pair of basketball shorts Lana had stolen from Drake the year before. I knew she had some of his clothes and found them easily in her pajama drawer.

Although I didn't find Linc or Dallas in the kitchen, there was a note on the coffee pot, scribbled in what had to be Dallas's curvy writing. I frowned as I lifted the yellow sticky note.

Glad you had fun with the rocker! Didn't take you for a screamer, Harp. Haha. But anyway... Keep your phone off, okay? Mommy dearest has been calling all morning. She and the evil stepbitch are in town again and want to suck up your happy feelings.

As I read the last line of the note, the cordless beside the coffeepot on the counter rang. My mind on what Dallas had said in the note, I didn't even bother to think about who could be calling as I lifted the phone to my ear. "Hello?"

"Linc?" a female voice I didn't recognize questioned.

"Nope. This is Shane. Linc isn't here right now." I turned around just as Dallas came walking into the kitchen. Her hair was a mess and the pajamas she wore looked like they were about three sizes too big. "Can I take a message?"

"Oh, no. I don't want to talk to Linc anyway." The tone was sweet and young sounding. "Would Harper happen to be around?"

"Nope again." I was pretty sure who was on the phone, having read Dallas's note. "But this is her boyfriend, so I'll be happy to let her know you called."

A fist hit my arm and I shot Dallas a glare, rubbing at the sore spot she had just made. Fuck, that girl didn't play fair... "Don't go there!" she whispered fiercely.

I ignored her. The silence on the other end of the phone was noticeable. "Hello? You still there?"

A sweet laugh, one that sent a chill down my spine came over the line. I knew that kind of laugh well. Sociopathic bitches had warmed my bed for so many years which made me an expert. "Yes, sorry. You just surprised me is all. So... Harper has a boyfriend? My little stepsister didn't mention you the last time I spoke with her."

I bet! "We haven't been dating that long, so she probably hasn't had the chance."

"Well then, we have to get together and get to know one another. I am just dying with curiosity about you." Dallas was slinging coffee mugs around now, and I shot her a look that told her to be quiet. Of course she ignored me! "You should have dinner with me and Mother tonight. And make Harper come too, darling. I didn't get to see my sweet sister the last time I was in town and I'm only in town for a few more days…"

"Sure." I told her the name of the restaurant that I knew Harper liked and asked her to meet us at seven. "Sound good?"

"Fantastic!" Ariana Calloway cried. "See you tonight, darling."

I replaced the phone and picked up my coffee cup. "Stop talking to yourself," I said.

"You have no idea what you just did, do you?" she exploded. "Way to fuck up a good thing, rock star!"

I froze, her words squeezing at my heart for some reason. "What's that supposed to mean?"

"It means that as soon as Harper finds out that you are having dinner with Ariana and Monica you will be out the door so fast your head will spin," she assured me. "News flash, stupid! Harper's mom and evil stepsister are only after one thing. To hurt and humiliate Harper to feel good about themselves."

I had already guessed that much. I knew that Harper had a self-esteem problem, knew that someone had—and still—made her feel like she wasn't beautiful. After reading Dallas's note to Harper, I now knew exactly who it was that had filled her head with such bullshit. And just as I had promised myself, I was going to rip them apart for doing that to her. "I'm not going to let that happen."

"Oh yeah?" Dallas demanded, but I saw a flash of something like hope mixed with a little admiration in her blue eyes.

"Yeah." I took a long swallow of my coffee then sat the mug aside. "Just don't tell Harper about that call, okay? I'm going to deal with this once and for all."

Harper

I was pulling on my sandals when my phone rang. I frowned at the screen then had to swallow my squeal of delight and excitement when I saw who it was from.

During the last few weeks I had been getting more and more offers from *Rock America* for freelance jobs. But the last time I had talked to the editor, he had told me that he had a position opening up and that he was really considering me for the job. I hadn't really let myself think about it simply because I didn't want to get my hopes up.

But if he was calling me now that had to mean something major... Right?

I picked up my phone and hit connect, my heart shaking my chest from excitement.

Rock America was a major magazine that was published monthly but also had web publications weekly. The magazine was based in California, but its journalists could work from anywhere. The editor told me again how much he liked my work, especially my photos. Then he made me an offer I really couldn't turn down...

Fifteen minutes later I left my room feeling as if I was walking on air. I wanted to tell Shane and share my news. When I found him in the kitchen with Dallas, some of my excitement evaporated. I could feel the tension in the air, knew that they had been arguing. Dallas and Shane normally got along well.

"What's going on?" I asked, standing in the kitchen doorway and glancing from my best friend to my boyfriend.

I saw the hard look that Shane gave Dallas and the glare she shot at him before forcing a smile. "Nothing. Just being my usual morning bitchy self."

Knowing my friend like I did, that excuse more than explained the tension in the air. I could only imagine the treatment Shane had to withstand while I was talking to my new boss. "Try not to bust his balls so much," I told her with a warning frown.

"I'll do my best," she assured me with a grin, which told me that she wasn't going to try at all.

Rolling my eyes at her, I crossed to Shane and wrapped my arms around him. "Guess what?" I commanded with a grin.

I felt the tension leave him and he dropped a kiss on the end of my nose. "What, baby?"

"I just accepted an offer from *Rock America*!" I squealed.

"Baby, that's great." He pulled me close, holding on tight. "I knew you could do it!"

"That's great news, Harp!" Dallas exclaimed from across the kitchen. "We should celebrate."

"Yes, definitely." I nodded, liking the idea. "Maybe drinks later?"

"After a celebration dinner." Shane kissed my lips lingeringly, and I almost forgot what we had been talking about by the time he pulled back. "I want to take you out."

Behind me I heard Dallas mutter something under her breath and then she spoke up. "Linc and I will meet you two later at the club then."

"Sounds good." I shot her a smile. "We're going to check on Lana. Want to come?"

"No, not right now. But tell her I will stop by later. Text me if there's anything she needs and I'll bring it with me."

Chapter Rock Fourteen

Harper

Making sure Lana was still doing well was at the top of my priorities. Of course I shouldn't have worried about my friend. When we walked into her private room an hour later, she was snuggled up in bed with Drake beside her.

It was kind of bitter sweet to look at them. They looked so content to be in one another's arms, but so sad too. The loss of their baby was hitting Lana hard, and I ached for my friend.

Shane had stopped in the gift shop and picked up a load of balloons that had Lana smiling as she watched him fight with the dozens of strings attached to them. He was melting my heart, watching the way he was so tender with his *sis*, as he liked to call Lana.

We had only been there about half an hour when Layla and Emmie joined us. Layla was all about Lana, making sure she wasn't in any pain. Shane took Emmie out into the hall for a long while, but I didn't question either of them when they returned separately. Shane just kissed my cheek and pulled me close.

I was pretty sure that I was in love with this rock star, and that didn't scare me like it might have a month ago.

We left the hospital later that afternoon and returned to my apartment to get ready for dinner. It was still too early to go out, but that was the excuse I gave Shane when I tugged him from Lana's crowded hospital room. I knew that Lana was going to be taken care of, and I needed some alone time with Shane before we went out later.

As soon as we walked through the front door, I was already tugging at his T-shirt. He made a growling noise and lifted me effortlessly into his arms. "I hope you aren't too sore from last night and this morning because I really don't think I can be gentle, beautiful."

I grinned at him as he practically jogged through the apartment toward my room. "Good."

As soon as the bedroom door was shut and locked behind us, he tossed me on the bed and jumped in beside me. The bed bounced, causing me to giggle. The giggles quickly died when his lips captured my own.

Even as he devoured me with his sensual lips, he was stripping me with his talented hands. Sneaky fingers tormented me, pinching my sensitive nipples and spreading the lips of my sex but not entering me. I didn't have time to think, could barely comprehend what I was feeling before he made me feel something more mind blowing.

His hot mouth left mine and swallowed one of my tiny breasts, making me cry out in pure elation. Fingers found my throbbing clit, making me whimper for more. I could feel my sex flooding with proof of my arousal, dampening my thighs and his hand.

"Fuck, baby!" he exclaimed when he felt how ready I was for him. "You are drenched." I watched as he licked his lips like a man dying of thirst. "I'm going to eat you until you beg me to stop."

Shane's mouth was on me before he even finished speaking. My body was his for the taking, my hips arching up to meet his seeking tongue. Strong fingers gripped my hips, holding me in place as he buried his face in between my wet folds. I lost control fast, my climax washing over me within less than a minute of his tongue working me over.

I was helpless to stop the small screams that escaped me as I fell apart, but he wasn't finished with me. His tongue never stopped, only intensifying my orgasm, pleasuring me through the peak. As soon as I fell off the edge of the precipice, he was working me toward another one. My fingers fisted the covers, holding on as he pushed me harder and faster toward the abyss of pleasure that awaited me on the other side of a second climax in as many minutes.

I cried out his name when I fell again, the orgasm lasting longer this time. Still, he didn't stop but added his fingers to the equation. Two thick fingers thrust into me as his mouth sucked on my clit. The growling noises he was making letting me know that he was enjoying the taste of me only made me wetter for him.

"Shane!" My voice was broken, hoarse from the screams that he had ripped from me with the two orgasms he had already given me. "I want you, Shane!"

"Not yet." His voice was rough, raspier than I'd ever heard it. "I love the taste of your need for me. Want more of it, baby. Give me more!"

His words only made me come apart fast as he flattened his tongue against my clit and held it there as he finger fucked me. I came for the third time and he ate it all up. Finally, he lifted his head and I could see my desire damp on his face. Maybe I should have been embarrassed, but I wasn't. Not with Shane, who had awoken all of this passion in me.

I watched as he sucked his bottom lip into his mouth. His groan stirred something deep between my legs back to life again. "I hope you liked that, baby. Because I plan on doing it often."

I didn't know how to respond to that, so I didn't. Instead, I grabbed his arm and pulled him down on top of me. "I want you inside of me. Now."

The way his eyes darkened only increased my need for him. "Whatever you want, beautiful."

His clothes were gone in seconds, and he was finally on his knees in front of me, naked and aroused and beautifully male. I grasped his dick with both hands, loving how he felt against my fingers. Hot, hard, silky. Spreading my legs wider for him, I guided him to my entrance.

Balancing his weight on his wrists now, he paused as the head of his big cock entered me. "I'm yours, Harper. And you are mine."

I blinked, unable to understand his words at first. "What?"

"I belong to you. Tell me you know that."

My breath felt like it was trapped in my lungs all of a sudden. "Shane... I..."

"I love you, baby."

Tears burnt my eyes and I quickly blinked them away. "Don't say that."

"Why not?" he asked softly.

"Because... Because..." I broke off, not completely sure why he shouldn't say those words to me. "Because I want to believe you."

A smile teased his lips. God, I loved it when he smiled. I felt like everything in the world was perfect when he smiled at me. "Believe it, beautiful. I love you."

Heart pounding, I covered his mouth with my hand. "Prove it."

He did. For hours he showed me by making love to me until I was sure I was going to expire from the sheer pleasure of it all.

After an afternoon full of nothing but lovemaking, all I wanted to do was sleep until it was time to meet Dallas and Linc later that night. I was sure that Shane and I had more than celebrated my new job, but he had other plans.

"Get your sexy ass up!" he commanded, jumping out of bed with more energy than I would have thought possible after just spending hours proving that he was indeed a sex god.

I groaned and rolled over, hiding under the covers. "Sleepy."

A firm slap to my bottom made me squeal. "Get up and shower or I'll do it for you."

When I didn't bother to move, he lifted me, covers and all, and carried me into the bathroom. I struggled in his hold, laughing and kicking. "Shane! Put me down!"

Suddenly, I was on my feet in the shower and the covers were stripped away from me. His mischievous smile made me melt for him all over again. "Do I need to wash you too?"

I gave him a mock glare. "Tyrant."

Laughing, he turned for the door. "Better get to washing, beautiful. I'll be back in five minutes."

Forty-five minutes later we were stepping out of the back of a town car and into one of the most extravagant restaurants in New York City. Luckily, I had dressed with this possibility in mind because I knew that Shane liked these types of places just as much as he liked little mom-and-pop eateries.

There was a line but when Shane approached the hostess and gave his name the woman told him his party had already arrived. I frowned up at him. "Are your friends joining us?" It didn't bother me if they were, but I'd thought it was going to be just the two of us.

I saw something like uncertainty flash across his face for a moment. He turned to me and cupped my face tenderly in his big, callused hands. "I love you, Harper."

"Shane…"

"Just trust me… Okay?"

His words only confused me, so I said nothing as he took my hand and linked our fingers as the hostess showed us to our table. The place was full of familiar faces, none of whom I knew personally but from celebrity gossip pages instead. Some of them turned to watch as Shane pulled me through the masses, others didn't find us interesting enough to bother.

I was too concerned about what Shane could have possibly meant to care or to notice the two women sitting at one of the best tables in the restaurant, watching us make our way toward them. It wasn't until we were mere feet away from them that I realized my mother and stepsister were about to pounce.

Shane

I felt Harper stiffen beside me and knew that she had spotted her family. Dallas' warning that I could possibly lose the best thing to ever happen to me echoed in the back of my mind. My stomach clenched with what could only be fear, but I pushed through it.

If I was to understand the girl I intended to spend the rest of my life with, we had to deal with this now.

Harper suddenly stopped and I was forced to turn and face her. My heart ached at the sight of her pale face and the hurt shining at me through those glasses I loved so much. "I don't want to be here," she whispered so softly I had to strain to hear her.

My fingers tightened around hers, and I bent my knees so that we were on the same eye level. "Why?"

She glanced over my shoulder for a moment, taking in her mother and stepsister. Before my eyes I saw her transform from a scared little kitten to a very sexy, very angry tigress. Her jaw clenched and those incredible violet eyes grew cold. I wasn't confident that was a good thing, but at least she no longer looked like a kicked puppy.

"Let's get this over with," she bit out in a voice that told me I was not her favorite person any longer.

Knowing that I had hurt her hurt me twice as much. In that moment, I was ready to take her away from there and beg for her forgiveness. I could only pray that Dallas wasn't right and that I wasn't about to lose the beautiful creature before me. "We don't have to stay," I rushed to tell her. "We can go home. Make love. Forget that this ever happened."

"No. You obviously had a reason to set this up." I wish I knew what she was thinking behind those now arctic purple eyes of hers. "I'm not sure I care what that reason was, but whatever."

She jerked her hand from mine when I tried to keep hold of it and pushed past me. I swallowed hard and pulled my phone from my dress pants. A rapid texted message was all I had time for before I turned and stepped beside Harper.

Monica and Ariana Calloway looked more like mother and daughter than Harper and her mom. Sure, the two other women were beautiful with their designer label dresses and makeup perfectly applied. Both had dark blonde hair that was obviously from a bottle. It couldn't compare to Harper's natural caramel hair. A glance at

Monica told me that Harper must have gotten her eyes from her father because hers were a kind of muddy brown that weren't even close to interesting. Their makeup was so thick it looked like if they smiled the wrong way their faces would crack.

As I stepped behind Harper I was overwhelmed by the very expensive—very French—perfume that the two women wore. As a kid I had suffered from asthma and the feeling of being unable to draw fresh air came back with a vengeance for a moment. When I could finally breathe, I found two sets of eyes on me: one hungry, the other disbelieving.

"This is your *boyfriend*?" Monica demanded.

The very tone of her voice made my hackles rise. I had planned on a simple dinner where I found out what the deal was with Harper and her mother. I could already make a small guess and was hating the bitch standing before me more and more with each passing second.

"Boyfriend?" Harper's tone was still cold. "Is that what you call the guy that warms your bed?"

Her words were a stab to my heart, but I knew that I deserved it.

Monica sucked in a shocked gasp. "Harper! You don't say things like that in public. I swear, that Dallas has really ruined you."

"No, Dallas saved me," Harper corrected her mother.

I felt a cool hand touch my arm and glanced down to find Ariana had moved closer. "Wow. Shane Stevenson. I never thought Harper would be able to get the most talked about sex god of rock and roll to look twice at her."

The way she looked up at me through her fake lashes with those blue eyes of hers was supposed to be sexy. And maybe two months ago I would have quickly taken the blatant invitation being offered with that smile of hers. But Harper was the only female that could even make my dick twitch. I covered her hand on my arm and pushed it away. The coy look left her face, and her cheeks heated with a mixture of anger and embarrassment.

"Harper is everything I've always wanted. Beautiful inside and out. Unlike some of the fake bitches I see right now."

Harper pulled a chair out and sat gracefully, leaving us all to follow suit. I took the seat directly beside her and attempted to catch her hand. She pulled away and clasped her hands together in her lap as the other two women took their seats. A waiter appeared and offered a wine list. I ordered a bottle of Harper's favorite white wine and a bourbon for myself, knowing I was going to need it.

"Well, Harper," Monica lifted her water glass and took a sip before continuing, "tell us how you met this…charming young man."

"He's Lana's brother-in-law."

"Ah." Monica grimaced in distaste. "I see."

"How is dear Lana?" Ariana asked, her tone full of sarcasm. "And the rest of your roommates."

"Fine." Harper's answer was pointed, leaving no room for follow up questions.

"There is no reason to be so snippy, Harper," Monica scolded. "Your sister is only being nice."

"Stepsister," Harper snapped.

"What is wrong with you? You never talk to me like this."

Harper raised a brow at her mother. "You mean I usually say nothing while you and Ariana sit and tell me how awkward I am. How I will never compare or be beautiful. Sorry, Mother. Shall I sit here and shut my mouth now? Maybe I should offer suggestions? I have gained two pounds since you last saw me. Ready, set, go!"

All of Harper's self-esteem issues clicked for me.

For so many years I'd seen the effects of the physical abuse on Emmie from her mother. Now I was understanding that abuse didn't always leave bruises that were visible. Some broke the soul and, in this case, destroyed a person's feeling of self-worth.

Well fuck that!

"You are evil bitches."

"Excuse me?" Monica demanded in a haughty tone. Gods, her soul was ugly when she got that look on her face, as if she thought she was better than everyone around her.

"I said, you are evil bitches." My gaze went to the clone sitting beside her, letting Ariana know that I was including her if she hadn't gotten that message yet. "I don't know what your problem is and, really, I don't give a fuck. You are one of those women that get off on making others feel less than they really are so you can feel better about yourself because you know that you will never be beautiful."

"I am beautiful." Monica sounded so sure of herself as she gave me a sneer in disgust.

"Sure you are. It only takes a gallon of paint and a few grand of designer clothes to make you that way. Meanwhile, your daughter has true beauty. She doesn't need the makeup, or hooker perfume, or clothes to make her stand out. You only wish you were that beautiful, and that's why you can't stand it. So you bring her down so that she thinks that she can't compare to you and Miss Thing over here."

"I'm a model!" Ariana argued.

"Who the fuck cares?" The tables around us grew quiet and I realized I had spoken louder than I had intended, but I didn't care. "You're a model, good for you. I'm a rock star, bitch."

Emmie

After getting a text from Shane, I wasted little time. Leaving Mia with Layla and Jesse, I grabbed Nik and pulled him out the door.

It had taken ten minutes to get to the restaurant by taxi. When we walked into the exclusive eatery, I ignored the hostess and headed for the table that I'd reserved for Shane earlier that day. From the look of the other patrons, Nik and I were severely underdressed in jeans and T-shirts. I hadn't known what Shane had planned, only that he was meeting Harper's mother. Of course, Lana had told me a few hours ago that Harper and *Mommy Dearest* weren't exactly a happy match.

Nik was right behind me as we walked through the dining room. I heard the murmurs of other diners, mostly the females, as they realized who Nik was. Sighs and giggles reached my ears, but they didn't bother me like they once had. I was more confident in Nik's love for me these days.

I spotted Shane at his table and could tell right away that there really was a problem. Shane was running his mouth, his face almost purple with his temper as he spoke loudly to the two women across from him. Meanwhile, Harper was just sitting there like a statue. She looked pale, and there was something in the set of her shoulders that told me she was less than amused. The way she was looking off in the distance made me wonder if she was even aware of the conversation going on around her.

"...I'm a rock star, bitch!" Shane's words filled my ears and I rolled my eyes. Whatever was going on, it seemed more like a pissing contest than anything else.

"You're trash," came the retort of the older woman at the table that I assumed was Harper's mother. She looked nothing like the sweet girl I had met just a few days ago, so I had to make a guess.

Hearing that old biddy speak to my friend like that did nothing for my own temper. I stopped just behind Shane and glared down at the older woman that smelled like a perfume factory and looked like an advertisement for clown school with all the makeup she was wearing. My mouth opened and I wasn't even sure what was about to come out when a strong hand covered my lips.

I shot Nik a glare, but he just grinned down at me. "Sorry, baby girl. We want to stay and your mouth will get us kicked out."

Of course he was right, but that didn't mean I had to like it.

"High paid trash, actually," Shane informed the older woman with what sounded like a smirk in his tone. "With big connections. One phone call and that cushy modeling contract you have will no longer exist."

Oh, I liked that idea. I didn't know if Shane was bluffing or not, but I planned to follow through on it. Mentally, I rubbed my hands together in glee. Nik, seeing the wheels turning in my eyes, laughed and released me.

Before I could step forward, Harper stood. She murmured something about the ladies' room and hurried away. Shane started to follow her, but I put a hand on his shoulder. I felt some of the tension leave him when he realized that I had arrived. He knew I had his back and would always do so.

"Hey."

I grinned down at him. "Hi. I would ask how your evening is going, but I caught the last five seconds of your conversation." My gaze went to the two women seated across the table. "Why don't you show these two delightful ladies to the door while I go talk with Harper?" I suggested with frost in my tone.

"She's so upset…" Shane's voice cracked ever so slightly, making my heart squeeze for him.

"I'll be gentle," I promised. After everything that had happened with Lana, I had learned my lesson. It didn't matter that I had only been looking out for Drake. I should have treated Lana better. Unfortunately, it had taken her nearly dying for me to realize that…

Pushing those thoughts away, I followed after Harper.

The bathroom was empty except for the beautiful girl standing by the long sink frowning at her reflection. Shane had told me so much about her over the last month or so. I hadn't really believed him about her self-esteem problem until now. I mean really? She was gorgeous with her thick, silky caramel hair. And that body? Fuck, I would kill for that ass. And those eyes? I had to spend a good ten minutes on makeup to get that wide eyed, soulful look even behind those kick ass chic glasses.

"No offence, but your mom is a bitch," I told her.

She stiffened at the sound of my voice, and I watched her eyes fill with annoyance in the mirror. I didn't blame her. She probably thought I had come to put my two cents in. I was sure that Lana had vented to her friends about me, and I only respected Harper more for being loyal to Lana.

But instead of sounding annoyed, Harper's tone was just tired when she agreed with me. "Yeah, she's always been like that."

I sat down on the little sofa. I still couldn't understand why there was one in the ladies' room at these snotty ass restaurants but appreciated it in that moment. "I can relate. My mother was a real monster."

Harper turned to face me. "She told you on a daily basis that you were ugly and would never compare to your incredibly beautiful stepsister?"

"No, sweetie. She beat me daily. That is when she wasn't stoned out of her mind." I patted the spot beside of me on the sofa when Harper's face paled.

After only a small hesitation, she moved and sat beside of me. "I…I'm sorry."

"Don't be. That part of my life was over when she overdosed." And that was when my real life began on the road with my guys—my family, if not by blood then by choice. "There are different types of child abuse, though. And I think you were just as much a victim as I was."

Harper shook her head. "No, my life was perfect compared to yours…"

"So you enjoyed being called ugly?" I rolled my eyes at her. "Verbal abuse leaves wounds too, sweetheart." She clenched her jaw and I sighed, not wanting to argue with her. "So tell me about it. Tell me how it was growing up with that hag out in the dining room."

She was quiet for so long that I started to wonder if she was even going to talk to me, but then she grimaced. "Monica and my dad divorced when I was young. Neither of them really took an interest in me, not that I cared. Less than a year later, she married my stepdad. He had more money than my dad…but Cecil was sweet. He cared about me. Still does."

"That's great. I'm glad you have him. Shane's told me about him and the few times that you guys have gone out together."

Violet eyes flashed with surprise. "Really?"

"Of course. Shane is always talking about you. I'm seriously getting tired of hearing all about Harper Jones." I was only half joking because, really, I couldn't call Shane without having to hear about the girl.

"I knew Ariana even before my mom married her dad. Our mothers were best friends. I was being compared to her from birth, actually. But when she became my stepsister it got worse. Then she started the modeling and life went from bearable to not so great in the blink of an eye. Of course puberty sucked ass." She ran a hand through her hair. "I had horrible skin, thick glasses, and braces. Really, I was hideous."

I couldn't contain my snort. "That's just teenage years. They suck for us all, babe."

"Yeah, well it's hard when you're surrounded by perfect models and the attitude that goes with them," Harper informed me, and I tried to see it through her eyes. I had never really had a girl as a friend until I had met Layla, but I knew that teenaged girls were nightmares from the one year I'd spent in high school before I'd gone to live with the guys. Girls were truly evil. I could only imagine the horror of being surrounded by those types of girls that also got paid for their looks.

All of that on top of being told by the one person that should have been supportive but was nothing but negative would have given any girl a complex.

"Isn't your best friend one of those girls though?" Shane and Lana both had told me that Dallas was an ex model.

A small smile teased the corners of Harper's Cupid's bow mouth. "Yeah, but Dallas isn't like them. She never wanted to be a model. Her mom is even more of a nightmare than my own. She forced Dallas into beauty pageants back in Texas until she was discovered and her mom signed her life over to a modeling agency until she turned twenty-one."

"That sucks."

"It hurt Dallas a lot. She always dreamed of being a nurse. She's really caring under all that attitude."

"I believe you." I had actually really liked the other girl, her tattoos and piercings only drawing me to her more.

For a good twenty minutes I sat and talked to Harper. Then Shane started texting me, and I figured it was time to go out and let him work things out with this girl of his. I stood but Harper remained seated. "Come on, let's go out and have some dessert," I urged her. "I know you have a weakness for lemon cake."

She gave me a small smile that didn't quite reach her eyes. "You go. I just need another minute or two."

I shook my head. "He really is sorry, Harper. Shane cares about you and would never willingly hurt you."

Her jaw clenched and she didn't answer, but I wasn't going to get in the middle. Not this time. I had learned my lesson with Drake and Lana…

When I returned to Shane and Nik it was to find that Lady Tremaine and the ugly stepsister look alike were long gone. One look at Shane told me that he wasn't doing too great. His face was pale, his eyes glazed with a mixture of tears and alcohol. I sat down beside him and grasped his hands.

"Talk to me."

"I've fucked up. I played a game with my relationship with Harper and lost." He tossed back the last of what looked like bourbon in his glass.

I couldn't disagree with him. I'd seen for myself how upset Harper was, but that didn't mean he lost her. Just as I'd seen how upset she was, I'd seen a little deeper than the other girl had liked. Miss Harper Jones was in love with one of my guys.

Harper

I waited until the door was closed behind Emmie and then started counting. Slowly I reached one hundred and grabbed my purse.

Tonight had been a disaster!

All I wanted was to go home and hide under my covers. I felt like I was eleven years old all over again, wanting to hide from my mother and stepsister and the disdain I knew they felt for me. I had no idea why my mother hated me so much that she felt she had to constantly beat me down with her mean, vile words. Ariana was different. I knew all her reasons for hating me, and I hated her right back. Even if at one point in our lives I had hoped that we could be friends.

I was thankful that the bathrooms were close to an exit that most of the servers used as their entrance to work. I rushed outside and down the little alley to the street, my arm already raised to flag down a cab. A small part of me felt like I was being devious, sneaking out on Shane the way I was without so much as a goodbye, but I didn't think I could handle seeing him right then.

All day I had been on cloud nine. Half in love with a guy that treated me like I was the only thing that mattered to him. A job that I had only ever dreamed about waiting for me to step up and grasp with both hands. Now… Now I felt like a kicked puppy, that same feeling that I was always left with after seeing my mother. Only this time it was intensified by a thousand because Shane had set me up for that pain.

From the moment I had seen Monica and Ariana sitting at our table I had shut down and completely tuned Shane out. I was aware when he spoke, when he so much as moved beside me. But what he said had been lost in my numb mind. He had broken something inside me that I hadn't even known was so fragile, something I hadn't even been aware I had given him.

Trust. I had trusted him wholeheartedly.

And he had tricked me into meeting with my mother and stepsister tonight. For what gain? I was clueless to the answer. I knew that it wasn't because he wanted to meet the semi-famous model, Ariana Calloway. Shane had met his fair share of models much more beautiful and more popular than my stepsister.

The taxi stopped at a red light. Swallowing hard around the dry lump in my throat, I pulled my cellphone from my bag and called Dallas. It rang five times before going to voicemail. Figuring she was already at the club waiting to celebrate my new job, I just left a message telling her I wasn't going to meet her and Linc. I had a headache and was heading home to sleep it off.

It wasn't exactly a lie. My head was pounding. Turning off my phone, I threw it into my purse.

Traffic was hell. It took twice as long to get home as it had to get to the restaurant in the town car earlier that evening. When the cab finally stopped in front of my building, I tossed the driver all the cash I had in my purse. It must have been enough, plus a decent tip, because he didn't argue when I stepped out and headed toward the front door.

Curtis, the night doorman greeted me, but all I could manage was a weak smile as I stepped into the thankfully waiting elevator. It only took a few moments to get to the twelfth floor, but my head was really starting to ache so it felt longer. When the elevator stopped, I stepped out, my attention on getting my keys from my purse.

"I'm sorry!"

My head snapped up at Shane's voice and I stopped. It hurt to look at him, but I did. His dinner jacket was gone, his once white shirt soaked in his sweat. He was panting and I knew that he must have run all the way from the restaurant. A glance at his once perfect

Italian shoes told me that he had scuffed them up to the point of ruin after running that distance in them.

I couldn't find the words or even the will to yell at him. I was equal parts hurt and in awe. What had been the point of tonight? To see if I was breakable? If that was the case, then the answer was a definite *yes*.

Strong, sweat dampened arms wrapped around my waist, pulling me into his hot body. He tucked my head under his chin, and I pressed against him. His heart was racing as fast as a champion race horse in my ear. Those strong arms actually trembled as he tightened them around me.

"I'm so sorry."

Still, I didn't speak. My vocal cords felt paralyzed, so I just let him hold me for a while longer.

I wasn't sure how long we stood there like that, but Shane finally stepped back and took my keys from me. I felt cold, lost, and alone those few seconds he was gone from me. He opened the door to the apartment and turned back to me. I saw the glassiness in those blue-gray eyes as he lifted me like I was a fragile glass doll and carried me inside.

My eyes had been dry all evening, but now as he gently carried me into my apartment and then to my bedroom, I felt my eyes fill with scalding tears. A broken sob escaped me and I felt him tense.

Tenderly, Shane placed me on my bed. I watched through my tears as he tore his shirt off and then came back to me. His eyes were bright and it shocked me when I saw a tear escape. It rolled down his cheek and fell, landing on my own cheek.

"I'm sorry, beautiful," he whispered.

"Wh-why?" I finally got out in a hoarse voice.

"Why what, baby?"

"Why did you do that?" The question exploded from me. "What did you have to prove?"

He closed his eyes, shaking his dark head. "I don't even know any more. It all kind of clicked into place when I talked to your stepsister this morning. No matter how many times I tell you that you are the most beautiful thing I have ever seen, you never believe me. I realized that Ariana and your mom must be behind all of that." He sucked in a shaky breath and another tear escaped his eyes. "I thought I could make you face your demons and prove to you that no matter what you will always be breathtaking to me."

Shane swallowed hard and broke my heart a little more as the tears began to fall faster. "But all I proved to you was that I'm a dick."

With trembling fingers I wiped his tears away. I couldn't disagree with him. Tonight had not been good for us. But for just a moment, a really small moment, I had done something I never had before. I had stood up to my mother. Crazy enough, she and Ariana were the only two people in the world I cowered to. They had this insane power to make me feel weak.

And tonight, I had stood my ground—for about five seconds—but still I knew it was Shane standing beside me that gave me even that little bit of courage. It had also shown me something that scared the living hell out of me.

Monica and Ariana no longer had the power to destroy me.

Because Shane now held all of that precious power in his big, calloused hands.

Chapter Sixteen

Shane

When I realized that Harper had left the restaurant, I knew I was on the very edge of losing her. Terrified didn't even begin to describe how scared I was. I left Emmie and Nik still sitting at the table for four and rushed outside.

When I didn't see her on the streets, I wasted no time calling Dallas in a desperate hope that Harper had went in search of her friends. Getting the other girl's voicemail had made my fear rise a few levels, and I just started running. Ten blocks later I was tossing my jacket at some homeless guy I had seen in a side alley because it was slowing me down.

The streets of New York were always crowded, but tonight they had been especially so. I had to push through the masses that slowed me down, not caring that I left people cursing at my back. By the time I got to Harper's apartment and questioned the night doorman, she still hadn't returned.

I was thankful that Lana had put me on her list of approved guests. The guy didn't stop me when I stepped onto the elevator. I was determined to see Harper tonight, even if I had to camp out in front of her door all night.

Now, as I stared down at the beautiful creature lying beside me on her bed, I realized something I should have already known. I could tell her I loved her a million times, but that would probably never register as the truth for her. I needed to show her, prove to her as well as say the words… And after tonight I was sure that I had only proved the complete opposite.

Blinking back my tears, I brushed a soft kiss over her forehead. I felt her tremble ever so slightly and knew that despite the disaster that tonight had been, she still wanted me just as much as I wanted her. "Can I make love to you?" I whispered, praying that she wouldn't push me away.

I watched as she swallowed hard, but after only the smallest of hesitations, she nodded. Some of the pressure around my heart eased, and I felt like I could take a deep breath for the first time that evening. I didn't give her time to think about her decision; I simply set out to prove to her how much I loved her with the one thing I knew I couldn't get wrong.

Just as tenderly as I had kissed her, I undressed her.

I brushed another kiss over her forehead, still tenderly but with all the love I felt weighing down on me. I inhaled the scent of her shampoo and was intoxicated by that delicate scent that reminded me of Harper. My lips trailed across her cheek to her jaw, lower to her neck, and over her collar bone.

I didn't go near her lips, refused to get too close to those sensitive breasts of hers. Right then all I wanted was to show her that I worshiped her body. If I let myself explore her hot mouth, or even those beautiful tits of hers, I would be just as lost as she would be. And this wasn't about losing our heads. This was about loving Harper.

I kissed across her right shoulder and down her arm, delighting in the little goose bumps that popped up on her sweet smelling skin. While my lips left no place untended, my fingers were busy tracing every feminine line of Harper: down her hips, her outer thighs, and over her calves to her ankles. Her skin was smooth, perfect. I loved the feel of it under my rough hands.

I grasped her feet with both hands, massaging the arches until she groaned with pleasure. Slowly, I kissed my way down her body until I reached her tiny feet. My tongue licked over the little ball at her ankle, making her jerk in pleasure that neither of us knew was possible. Her toes curled in my hands, and I knew that she was aching for something only I could give her.

I took my time. There was no rush as I kissed my way back up her legs. When I reached her knees, I urged her thighs apart. She spread willingly for me, like a flower blooming in the morning sun. My breath was trapped in my lungs as I looked down at the gorgeous woman before me.

This girl was my destiny. Now I just had to prove it to her.

Her thighs were like silk. They quivered with need under my fingertips, making my dick strain against the fly of my dress pants. I ached for her on a level that was nearly terrifying, but this wasn't about me and my needs. This was for Harper.

Harper

The first brush of the pad of his finger over my wet sex made my back arch. After the gentle seduction of his lips and hands on every part of my body, parts that I would never have imagined would be arousal points. I felt like a finely strung instrument. With the single touch of his finger to my clit, I went falling over an edge I wasn't even aware I was standing on.

"Ssshhhaaannneee!" I screamed his name, my body bucking uncontrollably.

"I love you, Harper," he whispered at my ear as he lowered himself beside me and kissed my lips until my body was calm once more.

For a long while all he did was hold me after that amazing orgasm. My heart was beating so fast that it felt like it was going to beat me to death, my breathing coming in little pants as I tried to come down off the high Shane had given me with the release.

When I could finally think more clearly, I felt how tense he was against me. His erection like steel pressing into my hip as it pulsed and twitched against me. My head slowly rose until I could meet his gaze and I saw how much it was costing him to just lie there holding me. He was in pain and I couldn't stand that thought.

The very idea that he needed me had my body melting. The release I had just experienced only intensified the renewed desire burning between my thighs. I wrapped my arms around his neck and pulled his head down to mine.

He didn't hesitate to kiss me back, didn't protest when I started unbuttoning his dress shirt, but he didn't help me either. I realized then that he was making this all about me. If I chose to lie back down and go to sleep, he wouldn't say a word. If I got up and left he wouldn't follow. For some reason that touched something deep in my heart.

Licking my lips, I smiled up at him. "Tomorrow, I want you to take me shopping."

I could see that my words had surprised him, but he simply nodded. "Whatever you want, it's yours." Those raspy words were like a vow that healed some of the damage tonight had inflicted on my heart.

The smile turned into a grin as I pushed his shirt off his shoulders and started working on his belt. "Whatever I want, whenever I want it?" I murmured, hoping I sounded seductive.

I must have succeeded from the way his dick twitched against his pants. "Yes."

With the belt undone, I unsnapped his pants and carefully pulled down the zipper, knowing that my man didn't like underwear. His erection sprang free, making my mouth water for a taste of him. And I would, I promised myself. I would suck his dick for as long as I wanted and he wouldn't stop me.

"I want you to buy me toys," I told him, glancing up at him through my lashes. I knew that my eyes drove him crazy and planned to use them to their full advantage tonight. "I want you to buy them for me, these sexy little toys, and I want you to use them on me. I want to play and experiment, and when we're both exhausted from all of that, I want you to make love to me… Can you do that for me, Shane?"

My heart pounded while I waited for his answer. I hoped he knew what I was telling him by asking for these things, prayed that he realized I was giving him my trust one more time, one last time. By asking him to experiment sexually, I was giving him everything.

"Y-yes," he whispered brokenly, and I lowered my head to take him into my mouth.

The taste of his pre-cum was addictive. I loved that sweet, slightly salty, tangy taste on my tongue. I sucked him in deep until his dick hit the back of my throat and made me gag. He groaned, enjoying the fill of my throat contract around the head of his thick cock. I pulled back and looked down at the bulging veins, examining them before tracing my tongue over every one of them.

His balls tightened and I gently grasped them with one hand, massaging, tugging, even moving lower to run my tongue over the delicate sac. Shane's fingers tangled in my hair, but he didn't urge me to take more into my mouth. He didn't do anything but hold my hair for me as I explored him.

This was for me.

I felt powerful, just as I suspected he wanted me to feel. By letting me have free rein tonight, by letting me do what I wanted when I wanted to his delicious body, Shane was turning over the only power he had. As I ran my tongue up the length of his silk covered steel dick, I raised my eyes to meet his gaze. Yes, I had all the power tonight.

Something told me that if I abused that precious power I would destroy this man. There was a vulnerability in his eyes that I wanted to know about. And I would find out. I would demand answers.

Tonight wasn't the time, though.

Our gazes still locked, I took him fully into my mouth, trying not to gag this time when the head of his cock hit the back of my throat. Breathing deeply through my nose, I took more of him, swallowing him inch by inch until I had all of him in my mouth. My tongue flicked over the base. When I had to come up for air, I pulled him from my mouth only to suck him deep again.

I could feel him getting close and knew that he was only moments away from emptying inside my mouth. With one last suck

I lifted onto my hands and knees and climbed over Shane. His fingers shook as he helped me fit his big cock into my tight, aching sex.

"I'll try to hold on," he promised.

I shook my head. "No. I want you to just let go." I slid down his length until he was as deep as I could take him. His girth stretched my inner muscles, making the pleasure almost unbearably intense.

Shane gritted his teeth. A dark vein pulsed on his neck, and I lowered my head to suck on it as I set a pace that I knew would send us both to Heaven shortly. Those strong, rough fingers of his gripped my ass, spreading my hips as he helped me. His breathing was labored, the air filled with his noisy pants. They mixed with my loud moans, filling the room with a symphony of our lovemaking.

I felt the first spray of his hot release hit deep within my womb at the same time his hands tightened on my ass and he tossed his head back.

"Harper!" he bellowed my name.

The world narrowed and all I could see, feel, hear were the effects of my own release. I cried his name, my hips moving faster as I tried to hold on to that powerful climax.

"Don't want it to stop!" I cried, desperate for the connected feeling I felt with him in that instant to stay just as much as I never wanted my orgasm to end.

He must have known what I wanted, must have needed it just as much. Even though he had just emptied himself deep inside of me, he was still rock hard. Groaning my name, he moved me onto my side. He pulled out only long enough to turn me so his front was to my back, and then he was filling me once more.

Strong arms came around my waist, anchoring me to him as he thrust into me from behind. Scalding lips kissed my neck, his evening beard scraping over the sensitive skin of my shoulder and ear. Fingers caressed over my quivering stomach until they found my clit, still sensitive after two incredible orgasms but ready for more.

"YES!" I cried when he rubbed my clit just the way I needed it.

The pounding of his dick deep inside me, the feel of his balls bouncing against my ass, added to his talented fingers on the bud of nerves—my sweet spot— all pushing me closer to a tsunami of an orgasm that would drown me when it hit.

"Come for me, beautiful!" Shane demanded in my ear in that raspy voice that I loved so much. "Come for me!"

My body was his to command. The wave swallowed me whole, left me gasping and struggling for air. My body shook, my inner muscles convulsing. Shane increased his pace, his balls slapping against my ass harder, and I rode out the last draining waves of an orgasm that left me nearly unconscious.

Shane

I hadn't been able to sleep deep since I was a kid, but that night I slept like the dead. How could I not after Harper and I had set the sheets on fire?

I fell asleep still inside of her, unable to find the strength to move once I had caught my breath. When I opened my eyes to the morning sun shining through her window, it was to find she was no longer beside me. Jerking into a sitting position, I glanced around for her.

"Hi," her sweet voice drifted to me from Lana's bed. Blinking, I focused on her. She was sitting crossed legged on the full sized bed, her camera in hand as she continued to take picture after picture of me.

"Hey, beautiful. What are you doing?" I cocked my head, not caring that I was completely naked and that she was still taking pictures of me.

A small smile teased her lips as she snapped another picture of me sitting on the edge of her bed. "I hope you don't mind. I couldn't resist. The sun was shining across your delicious body and I had to capture it."

"No, baby. I don't care." And to show her I meant it, I stood and stretched, giving her plenty of angles to capture. Her favorite? My front, especially the morning hard-on that I was sporting just for her.

After a few minutes I was ready for more than just to be the subject of her artistic eye. I wanted her maybe even more than I did the night before. How was it that I wanted her this much, and yet the need kept growing? It would consume me before long.

The camera fell from her hands and landed carefully on the bed next to her as I trapped her against Lana's mattress. All she was wearing was a camisole and a pair of panties. Neither of which stood much of a chance. I ripped the sides of her thin panties, loving the way she squealed in excitement as my fingers sought and found her damp pussy.

Her breath hitched in my ear letting me know that she was enjoying every second of my exploration. I thrust two fingers deep then pulled them from her and rubbed her arousal over her bottom lip before sucking them into my mouth. Fuck, I loved the taste of her!

Almost shyly, I watched as her little tongue darted out and skimmed over her bottom lip, tasting herself. Her lashes lowered, but not before I saw the reaction in those incredible, violet eyes. She liked it and was aroused by her own unique flavor.

"Tastes good, doesn't it, baby?"

Heat filled her checks but she nodded. I captured her lower lip with my own, sucking away the last of her honey. "You asked me last night to experiment with you. To guide you into the world of sex play. Do you still want that, beautiful?"

Again, she nodded and my heart doubled its already erratic rate. "I know what you are giving me, Harper. All of that trust I almost killed last night... Thank you."

"Please don't make me regret it," she whispered.

"No, never," I vowed. "I love you, Harper. That isn't exactly easy for me. Letting someone this close is terrifying." I pulled back a little, propping myself up on my elbow so I could look down at her. "Remember the first time I kissed you and ran?"

She flinched but didn't turn away from me as I had feared she would. "Yes..."

I raised a hand to push back a few strands of caramel hair that had fallen across her cheek. "It was because I was terrified of tainting your sweetness. My past... It isn't pretty, baby. And not just because of the rock and roll lifestyle I've led for so long. There are things that... I was just a kid, but..."

Trembling fingers gently covered my lips. "You could never taint me, Shane. Never. I already knew about the girls. Lana wasn't exactly unforthcoming about your background."

I kissed her fingers and carefully pulled them away. "No, I didn't think she would be." Harper hadn't cared about that and it only made me love her more. But it was the other things that I feared would leave her sickened by me. "When I was a kid... I was abused."

Violet eyes darkened. "Like Emmie?" she whispered.

I closed my eyes and shook my head. "No, baby, not like Emmie."

I still held onto her fingers, so I knew when she realized what kind of abuse I was alluding too. The warmth seemed to seep from her hand, the tips starting to tremble. Slowly, I opened my eyes to meet her gaze. The tears building in her sweet gaze tore me apart, her quivering chin breaking my heart.

"Wh-who?"

"My stepdad."

A sob escaped her and I pulled her against my chest. "No," she whispered. "No. I... I'm sorry!" I waited for her disgust but it never came. At least not disgust for me.

Over the next hour we talked about my past. For the first time in my life I told the whole story, something I hadn't even told Drake and Emmie. It was hard, for both of us, but we held each other as I got it all out. How Rusty had come to my room one night when Drake was gone for a week at band camp. The pain and humiliation of that horrible night...

"I hate to even touch myself," I whispered into her hair. "My hands are rough, like his were."

"So…" She paused and cleared her tear clogged throat. "You've never..?"

I shook my head. "Never."

Slowly, she raised her head. Her glasses were streaked with tears, and she took them off, tossing them on the bedside table. I watched, a little anxious as she moved to sit on the edge of the bed. Her hands combed through her long, caramel hair, and a shaky sigh escaped her. For a long moment she sat there, not moving, not speaking, and I grew worried that I had killed her desire for me.

But then she reached for the edges of her camisole and pulled it over her head, leaving her naked. When she turned around to face me, her eyes were bright with determination…and passion. "I want to erase all of those memories for you. I want to take away the pain."

Relief washed over me and I pulled her back into my arms. "You do that every time you are in my arms."

"Then I will have to make sure I never leave them." Her lips caught mine in perhaps the gentlest kiss we had ever shared. It took my breath away.

The kiss lasted forever, but I didn't want it to ever end.

Silky fingertips traced over my skin from my face to my waist, learning me like I had tried to learn her. When she broke the kiss, I felt lost for a moment before those hot, damp lips kissed a path down to my chest. Lips like satin settled over my heart, leaving me breathless for another reason altogether. Violet eyes rose to meet mine as she kissed my heart again. Just as she had given me her trust last night, I could see that she was giving me something even more special in this moment.

They weren't the words that I wanted to hear, but this would do. Seeing the love shining at me from those purple depths would definitely do!

Harper let her kiss trail lower, her little tongue dipping for a second into my naval, making me aware that she was indeed learning what I liked. Her perfect little tits brushed over my thighs, the hard nipples combing through the rough hair on my legs. Silky hair tickled across my abdomen as her head traveled lower, and I couldn't hold back the groan when her hot breath whispered over the head of my aching dick.

I reached for her hair, pulling it to one side so I could see her face as she kissed the tip of my weeping cock then slid her tongue down the length. Fuck! Could there ever be a sexier sight than this girl sucking on my cock?

When she reached the base, she sucked my balls into her mouth. There was a delicate *pop* as she released them carefully. "I want to kiss your hurt away."

All I could do was nod because my throat was suddenly too dry, too tight. There was no way of describing this moment between us. Sweet. Beautiful. Full of love and, yes, passion. But those words couldn't fully describe the feeling in my heart as she lowered her head and took me into her mouth. It couldn't come close to explaining how in awe I was. Harper kissed every inch of my cock, kissed and licked my balls until I didn't know if I was even still breathing.

She paused and took hold of my right hand. Her lips kissed my palm, the thick calluses left on my thumb from years of playing the guitar. I jerked as she guided my hand to my dick and cupped my fingers around the shaft.

"Look at me, Shane," she instructed in that soft, sweet voice of hers. "Don't look away."

The first guided stroke made me a little less hard, just a little. I wanted to look away, to let go of my dick, but her hold on me was stronger than those needs. Her fingers kept their firm yet gentle hold on mine and increased the pace of our strokes. That sexy as sin mouth lowered over the tip, and I went completely rock hard once more.

The sweetness of the moment was still there, but as she sucked me and guided me to jack the shaft of my dick, I went mindless. It felt so good, so fucking good. The pace was too slow and I increased it without her help, without her hand holding mine. I tightened my fist, pumping harder into the hot cavern of her mouth. My dick grew thicker and longer in my hand, and still I didn't slow the pace.

Harper raised her head and kissed me, holding on to my shoulders as I jerked myself off for the first time in my life.

I could feel the release building, and with a shout of her name I exploded. It sprayed over her stomach, but she didn't move away. Instead, she deepened the kiss, rubbing her stomach against mine as she spread my release over us both. We slid together perfectly and without even thinking about it, I thrust my still hard dick deep inside of her.

"Yes!" she cried, her head tossed back. Her hair flew back over her shoulders, leaving it wild and untamed. So fucking sexy! "Harder!" she commanded.

I sat up with her still in my arms, my dick deep inside her tight pussy. Her arms held on to my shoulders, and I cupped her perfect ass as I thrust faster. Her muscles contracted around my cock, letting me know that she was getting close. She was so hot, so tight, and I needed her to come for me before I could let myself join her.

I licked my finger and then skimmed it down her ass before gently thrusting it into her most forbidden of passages. Every muscle in her body seemed to contract, and I was rewarded with her pussy convulsing as she came apart in my arms.

"Shane!" The way she screamed my name drove me crazy. She scratched her nails over my shoulders and that pleasure filled pain sent me flying over the edge.

Chapter Rock Eighteen

Harper

While Shane showered I went in search of coffee and something sweet to eat. I was starving and couldn't remember the last time I had eaten. Dinner last night had completely killed my appetite, but after the morning Shane and I had just had, I was ravenous.

Dallas was sitting at the kitchen table when I walked in, her phone in hand as fingers moved with quick, sure movements. Her head snapped up when she heard me, and I saw the look in her eyes. She looked a little guilty and I realized that she must have known about Shane's dinner plans.

"Well…" I muttered as I crossed to the coffee pot and poured a bigger than normal cup. "You suck."

"I'm sorry, Harp."

"You should be. Don't you think you should have warned me what I was walking into last night, Dallas?" I demanded, turning to face her.

"No, because then you wouldn't have faced them. You would have just kicked his ass out." She grimaced. "And you really needed to deal with your mom, Harp."

I glared at her for another long moment before sitting down beside her at the table. "I know. I stood up to her last night…"

Dallas's eyes widened and then she grinned. "Good. I'm glad. You should have done that years ago."

"You still should have told me," I grumbled under my breath before taking another swallow of my hot coffee.

"I swear it won't happen again." Dallas tossed her phone aside, giving me her full attention now. "So, how did it go? I know the rock star is here. I think the whole fucking building knows that he's here after this morning. Things couldn't have gone that badly."

For the next ten minutes I told her all about the evening before. Dallas listened intently while I filled her in on the disastrous dinner, the arrival of Emmie, and then getting home to find Shane had run the entire way. When I was done, because there really wasn't anything she needed to know about what came after, Dallas shook her head. "Sounds like he has it bad."

"He says he loves me," I confided.

"Yeah, I know. I see it in his eyes." Dallas gave me a small smile. "Apparently not all rockers are complete douchebags."

I raised a brow, wondering about her own rocker romance. "How are things with Axton? Have you spoken to him since the other night?"

Slim shoulders lifted in a shrug and she grimaced again, causing her Monroe piercing to lift with the motion. "He's called and left a few texts, but I'm not really worried about answering him back. He really isn't worth my time."

"So you don't know if he really hooked up with Gabriella at that party or not?"

Dallas stood and went to the fridge to take out a bottle of diet Coke. "I know he did, so it doesn't matter. He loves her."

I didn't know what to think. I had seen Axton with Dallas only once, but I knew that he felt something stronger for her than just lust. Still, she knew him better than I did, so I wasn't going to put my foot in it. If Dallas wanted to call it quits with Mr. Rock God, then that was her choice.

My phone buzzed with an email, and I glanced down at it to find it was from my new boss. I frowned as I read the document and then muttered a curse. "Well there goes my plans," I grumbled.

"What?"

"My boss wants me to handle a story that someone else refused to do." I stood, coffee in hand. "I don't care, but good grief. A little more than an hour's notice would've been nice."

Shane was just coming out of the bathroom when I entered my bedroom. He had a pair of basketball shorts on and nothing else as he used a towel to dry his hair. "You look grumpy."

I blew out a frustrated breath. "Yeah, I kind of am. I have to work. Guess we won't be going shopping after all."

Shane tossed the towel aside and reached for me. Dropping a tender kiss on my lips, he let his hands rub down my back and over my hips. Strong fingers gripped my ass hard through my sleep shorts. "Don't be disappointed. I'll take care of everything, and we can do something tonight."

I smiled. "Yeah?"

"Yeah. We can't really go out to that kind of store, not without some tabloid picking up the story. I don't want you exposed to that shit, so we will have to go a more discreet direction."

I was curious now. "How so?" I thought we would just find a local porn shop and buy everything that looked like fun, but I was kind of clueless about what those things might be.

"Don't worry about it, beautiful. Just trust me to guide you." He kissed me, lingering for just a minute before stepping back. "Text me and let me know when you're finished and I'll pick you up. In the meantime I'll go check on Lana."

Curiosity ate at me all afternoon as I traveled uptown to the hotel where some band was staying today, and today only, before heading off for a three month long tour across the Midwest. The band proved to be difficult to question for the interview, but I somehow got through it and got some good pictures that I sent to my boss.

Shane texted me that he was on his way, and I started on the rough draft of my interview on my phone while I waited.

I had been sitting in the lobby awhile when a shadow appeared beside of me, and I raised my head to find the more difficult band member that I had just interviewed standing there watching me. It was a little unnerving, but I gave him a forced smile.

"Hi." I thought his name was Trey, but I couldn't be sure. He and the other band members of Drunken Monkeys had spent more time making sexual comments than answering the questions my boss had requested I ask.

"I was hoping you hadn't gone far."

I shrugged. "Nope, I'm waiting on my boyfriend to pick me up." I put a little more emphasis on the word boyfriend, hoping the jerk would take the hint and go away. He really gave me the creeps, even if he was kind of hot. Something in his hazel eyes just didn't set right with me.

There was an empty chair beside of me and Trey took it. He sat on the edge, leaning closer toward me as he spoke. "How about coming upstairs with me for a few hours? I really want to see what is under that cute little skirt."

"And I'm really trying hard not to puke." I glared at him. "Let's see who succeeds first, asshole."

A big, slightly beefy hand reached over and rubbed over my knee before I could move. "Don't play hard to get, pretty girl. You know I'm a sure thing."

I felt bile rise in the back of my throat as his hand touched my skin. Without thinking about it, I picked my keys and lifted the little can of Mace. One, two, three…

Trey, the Drunken Monkey screamed as the Mace entered his eyes. Jumping up, rubbing at his face, he started calling me all kinds of vile names. I tried not to laugh at him, really, I did. He was used to getting any girl to fall into bed with him and it had gone to his head. My first rejection must have sounded like a hard to get line, but my second more forceful rejection was hard to take in.

"What the hell is going on here?" A deep voice that never failed to send shivers through me had me raising my head.

The can of Mace was still in my hand. When Shane saw it and put that together with the reaction of the hurting rocker, his entire expression changed to something I had never seen before. And I hoped I never saw it again. His face contorted with a spasm of rage, and the next thing I knew Trey was lying on the floor of a five star hotel. He was no longer screaming in pain because Shane had knocked his ass out.

"You fucking asshole!" Shane yelled in the unconscious man's face. "Touch my girl again and I will break your fucking neck!"

He was shaking with rage, his face so red it was almost purple. I jumped up and grabbed his arm, afraid he would start kicking the other man.

"Hey, hey." I forced him to turn and face me. When my arms went around him, I could actually feel the rage fading a little. "It's okay. Nothing happened."

"Something obviously happened or you wouldn't have had to protect yourself!" Shane growled. "Fuck this, you are not going to any more interviews unless I'm with you."

I wanted to argue, but knew now—while he was still vibrating with anger—was not the right time. So I let it go for the moment.

On the floor, Trey groaned as he slowly came around. I turned so I was standing between him and Shane.

"What happened?" he mumbled as he glanced around. When his gaze focused on Shane, he blinked, his eyes obviously still stinging from the Mace. "Stevenson?"

"Yup." Shane's arms wrapped around my waist, staking his claim. "Stay the fuck away from my girl."

Trey muttered a curse. "I didn't know she was your girl, fucker. And really? You have a steady girl?" His gaze traveled to me and over my body almost leeringly. "Not that I can question your taste." But then he wiped his hands over his eyes. They were watering from the reaction to the chemical. "Fuck, this hurts!"

Because the lobby was off to the side of the hotel entrance, no one had noticed our confrontation. But with Trey continuing to curse it drew the attention of the manager and a few others. The manager, an older man with almost completely gray hair, stepped forward. "Is there a problem here?"

Shane turned to face the man. "The guy has something in his eyes," he informed the manager with a face that was like stone it was so hard. "He may need medical attention."

I glanced down at the other rocker. His face was red, the burn from the Mace affecting the skin around his eyes as well. I bit my lip, feeling sorry for the guy now.

"This doesn't look good at all," the manager commented when he crouched down to take a better look at the guy's eyes. "What happened, sir?"

I waited for the Drunken Monkey to tell the older man that I had assaulted him. I had a sudden fear that the cops were going to be called and I'd be arrested for spraying Trey with my Mace. Instead, he grumbled something about being stupid and left it at that.

Shane tightened his hold on my waist and urged me to move away from the group that was now forming around us. When we where outside in front of the hotel, he pulled me against him and kissed me hard. "I don't think I like your job anymore."

I gave me a small smile. "It's not so bad," I assured him. "And I carry my Mace for things like this."

"I'm buying you a Taser. You can fry the next guy's ass. Not that I see this happening again. No one will touch you when I'm with you."

I bit my tongue to keep from arguing with him but couldn't help but smile at how protecting and possessive he was.

Shane

I was still shaking a little by the time the taxi pulled to a stop in front of Sensual House. I couldn't get the thought of some guy trying to manhandle Harper out of my mind, and the more I thought about it, the more pissed I got. But my girl sure had shown some balls today.

I knew Trey from way back when Demon's Wings had first gotten started. He and the other Drunken Monkeys were hard-core, worse than Demon's Wings or even OtherWorld when it came to causing trouble and partying. There had even been a rumor a few years before that their drummer had raped an underage girl after one of their concerts. And I wasn't all that sure it was just a rumor.

So it was little wonder why I was so torn up over Harper's ordeal. But with her holding on to me the entire taxi ride, I was beginning to feel calmer. Simply having her hand on my arm was enough to ground me.

I paid the driver and then pulled her out with me. She frowned up at the huge brownstone building. It looked like any other place in the city and in beautiful condition on the outside with a nondescript look that was completely misleading to the business that was housed inside. Sensual House was one of several sex clubs that were located in New York. It catered to every possible sex fetish known to man, and some that weren't even invented yet.

I hadn't ever been to Sensual House before and knew that it was a more couple oriented place than what I usually went for. While most clubs catered to casual sex, Sensual House was exclusively for couples, couples that were experimenting or just needed to spice up their sex life. A place where both partners could feel safe and secure with the added anonymity.

When Harper had asked for toys to experiment with, I had known this was the place for us.

"Where are we?" she asked as she continued to stare up at the brownstone.

I didn't answer but pulled her up the steps and rang the doorbell. A woman answered the door with an air of professionalism to her. "Yes?"

"Shane Stevenson." I had called ahead to make arrangements for everything I wanted and needed for Harper's first time. My name and the password that each client was given was my key inside. "Red room."

The woman tilted her head and stepped back to let us enter. The foyer was typical of any business, clean and stylish in décor. Harper remained quiet beside me as the woman closed the door behind us. "Welcome to Sensual House, Mr. Stevenson. Your room is already prepared. My name is Yvonne. Should you and your lovely guest need anything, please use your in-room phone and we will be happy to assist you in any way."

I took the key that she offered and lead Harper upstairs. When we reached our room, I pulled her inside and finally explained where we were. Her eyes widened. A part of me had been worried that this would freak her out; that this wasn't something that she would go for. But as the surprise started to fade, I could see the hunger filling those violet eyes I loved so much.

Harper

I'll be honest, the whole sex club thing had really thrown me. But when I realized what Sensual House was about, I relaxed a little. I knew that Shane only wanted to make me feel safe and didn't want to break my trust. Oddly enough, he had set me at ease because as excited as I'd been, I'd also been scared.

The room we were in was just like something out of an erotic novel. Red walls with crimson décor. The four post king sized bed had actual silk sheets, and of course they were red as well. Pillows in red and black were stacked against the head board while rose petals—red rose petals—were scattered across the sheets.

And on a long table covered in a satin cloth, toys of every shape and form were ready to be played with. My nerves returned as I crossed over to them and touched one after another. I was completely naïve and knew absolutely nothing about any of these objects and could only take a guess what each did.

Strong arms wrapped around my waist from behind. Shane's hard chest was warm against my back. A breath shuddered from him, and I realized he was just as nervous as I was. That calmed all of my nervousness and I turned in his arms.

"Say something."

I smiled. "Thank you. This is perfect."

His eyes were searching mine, seeking reassurance that I was really okay with all of this. "Are you sure? We can leave right now and we can do this however you want, whenever you want."

"No. I think this is going to be fun. Besides, I trust you."

Relief flashed across his handsome face, and he kissed me long and hard. No matter how many times Shane kissed me, I would never be ready for how intoxicating his taste was. How just the skim of his tongue over my bottom lip sent a shiver down my spine and made my sex flood with desire. He took my breath away and left me aching with just a simple kiss.

Almost reluctantly he stepped back. "There is lingerie in the closet. I ordered a few that you can choose from. Pick what you want and model it for me."

There were three different sets of lingerie to choose from: a red and black lace chemise set that came with fishnet thigh highs and a garter belt; a crimson skirtini set that came with silk stockings; and a black satin peek-a-boo bra and thong set.

Pulling the skirtini set out, I went into the bathroom to change. The bathroom was gigantic. A walk-in shower was right next to a clawfoot tub that was easily big enough for two. A floor length mirror was on the wall in front of the shower, and I could easily imagine Shane making love to me in the shower while I watched in that mirror.

That image alone had me panting a little as I stripped of my simple black skirt and white top. The skirtini was cute, and I loved the feel of the silk stockings on my skin as I slid them over my legs. When I had dressed in the lingerie, I turned to get a glance of myself.

For the first time in my life, I thought I could actually see what Shane claimed he saw every time he looked at me. I might not be beautiful, but right in this moment I looked sexy as hell.

Smiling, I left the bathroom to find Shane sitting on the edge of the big crimson bed. He was actually wearing boxers, and that made me pause for a moment. My man looked really good in the masculine underwear.

He held his hand out for me, and I eagerly crossed over to him and placed my hand in his. Blue-gray eyes were eating me alive as they traveled from the top of my head to the tip of my silk stocking covered feet. A gentle tug and I was pulled across his chest as he fell back onto the bed.

"I love you so much, Harper."

"I love you too." It felt good to tell him. My heart felt lighter for having told him those magically powerful words. "Better not break my heart, mister," I gently teased, even as I was praying that he never would.

"I won't. Your heart is safe with me," he promised.

With a smile I brushed a kiss over his lips.

It was so crazy how one little kiss could light a spark that led to such a huge explosion. Shane stood and pulled his boxers down his powerful thighs. I licked my lips as his dick sprang free and lifted toward his stomach. I had come to learn the three stages of Shane's need for me: hard, harder, hardest. At the moment he was definitely reaching the hardest, and I grew wet when I saw the tip of his dick weeping for me.

"Did you see anything you wanted to try first?" His voice was all throaty, a sure sign that he was just as needy for me as I was for him.

I blushed and nodded. Shane smiled down at me tenderly. "Which one?"

I pointed toward the first toy, the one that had caught my attention the most. It was odd looking, as they all were, but this one looked the safest. Shane tilted his head and turned toward the large, unopened bottle of lubricant. I was in awe as he put a few squirts into his hands and rubbed them over his straining dick. He stilled for a moment as his rough fingers stroked over his sensitive flesh, and I realized that he still had that hang up despite our healing lovemaking that morning.

When his dick was shiny with the lubricant, he reached for the toy and slipped the ring part down over his shaft. He had to stretch it wide to fit, but when it was in place he looked nearly twice as big as he hand moments ago. My mouth went dry and my sex grew wetter. I had to squeeze my thighs together to ease some of the ache that was starting to consume me.

Shane squirted a small amount of the lubricant into his hand and came back to the bed. As he reached me, I caught the scent of the lubricant. "Lemon?" I said with a grin.

"Our favorite." He winked as he climbed onto the huge bed on his knees. The lubricant was room temperature, but my body was on fire so it felt a little chilly as he rubbed the thick liquid over my clit through the crotchless skirtini. "Don't want you to get friction burn, beautiful."

I moaned as his fingers lingered, warming the lubricant as he massaged it into my aching flesh. As good as this felt, I was ready to tell him to forget the toys. All I wanted was him. But before I could open my mouth, he leaned over me and kissed me. My thighs spread wider for him, and I whimpered as the tip of his slick dick slipped into me.

Nipping at my lip, keeping me distracted while he reached between us and pressed a button at the same time, he slipped completely into me. My finger nails dug into his back at the first feel of the vibrations on my clit. The sensation felt so good, so amazing, that it scared me for a moment. Shane didn't move as he let me become accustomed to the feel of the little vibrator that had pleasure nubs rubbing over my aching clit.

"Do you like this?" he asked in that desire roughened voice that never failed to send shivers down my spine.

"Y-yes. Oh, yes!" I gasped when he moved, causing the vibrator to glide across my clit while he gently thrust deep. "Oh, oh, I like this."

"Fuck, baby!" He buried his face in my neck. "Watching you like this is killing me! Come for me, so I can empty into you. I swear I will do it all over again. As many times as you want. Just please come with me now."

His words shattered me. My nails scraped across his back as my inner muscles clenched around his thick arousal. I felt the first hot, thick jet of his release and convulsed around him.

"AHHHHH!" I cried, coming apart for him harder than I could ever remember doing before.

Over the next three hours, Shane gave me one explosive orgasm after another, all with a different toy. I found that I loved playing with him like this and was almost scared that I'd become addicted to it. Breathless from another mind blowing release, I lay on top of Shane. We were both damp with sweat and borderline exhausted. With a growl, he held me close and I pillowed my head on his chest, comforted by the heavy pounding of his heartbeat.

"You are amazing," he murmured, kissing the top of my head.

"So are you."

"It's never been like this for me before," Shane confessed. "I've never felt like this."

Curious, I propped my head up on my hand. "How do you feel?"

"More alive. Free. Captivated and enthralled." He grinned. "I'm a little in awe of you and how much I love you, beautiful."

My smile wasn't as big as his as I tried to keep my sudden tears from spilling. "Me too. It's a little scary."

"No, baby. It is *crazy* scary, but that's not a bad thing." He pulled me back down so that I had my head on his chest once more. "Let's get some rest and play some more."

"You know, I really like it here."

"Good. I'm glad I didn't freak you out."

"Maybe we can try out a few of the other rooms next time."

He laughed. "Sure. Whichever one you want, beautiful."

Harper

The yelling woke me from a deep sleep.

It took me a good thirty seconds to realize where I was. Over the last several months, I had spent equal time in Shane's bed as I had my own. During that time I hadn't slept alone once, so I was even more confused because I was alone now.

Shane's raised voice brought me out of my confusion, and when I heard Lana join in, I became concerned. Since her miscarriage Lana's emotions had been all over the place, but she had started acting more and more like the old Lana. By the time Drake had proposed a month ago we were all sure she was going to be alright.

But the way she was yelling at the moment told me she was far from fine about something. I could actually hear tears in her voice as she yelled at Shane.

Tossing the covers back, I grabbed the robe I had been leaving at Shane's place. I was completely naked, but there was no time for more than the thin robe. I was just pulling it closed and tying it tight when I threw the door open and rushed down the hall to the living room.

The voices were louder now that they weren't muffled behind the thick door of Shane's bedroom. "I don't give a fuck what you say! There will be no bachelor party."

I froze in the entrance to the living room. Bachelor party? This was the first time I had heard anything about one, but of course I should have thought Shane would want to throw one for his brother. Still, I knew a little about the last *bachelor party* Shane and his brother had in Vegas just the year before.

"It isn't going to be like that!" Shane defended. "I swear to you, sis. This is just going to be a bunch of guys getting together and catching up."

"Which really means you are all going to a strip club. No."

Yeah, that was the picture that had invaded my mind the minute the words *bachelor party* had been mentioned. If I had a say in it, my answer would be a loud *no*, too. In the months that Shane and I had been dating, we'd been nearly inseparable. I hadn't even had one reason to be jealous of other women, but suddenly I was feeling very insecure.

"I told you, Lana. No strippers. No booze. Just OtherWorld and Demon's Wings getting together to jam and relax." Shane glared down at the woman that was going to become his sister-in-law in just a little over a week. "Don't be selfish, Lana. Drake deserves a party."

Lana gasped and I watched as the color drained from her cheeks. "Is that what I am? Selfish?" The hurt in her voice and shining out of her amber eyes twisted something in my chest. "So it's selfish to feel like this? To be scared out of my mind when it was one of your parties that nearly destroyed us in the first place?"

Shane flinched as if she had slapped him. "No! Look, I know you're scared. You have every right to be. But you have to trust him, Lana. He isn't going to hurt you again. Not when he has everything he could ever possibly want now."

"You know what? Fine! Go, have your fucking party. But that just means that I can have one of my own." Lana turned her head and meet my gaze. I saw the hurt, the defiance, and the vengeance burning in her eyes and had to bite my cheek to keep from grinning. "Right, Harper?"

Shane's head snapped around. His blue-gray eyes narrowed, but I didn't even look his way. "It's going to be epic," I assured my friend.

"Now wait a minute," Shane said as I moved past him to hug Lana.

But I tuned him out, already making plans for Lana's party. "Let's call Dallas. She will know exactly what to do. I'm thinking Emmie and Layla will want in on it too."

"Harper, it's not a traditional bachelor party!" Shane tried to explain as I picked up the cordless by the couch and punched in the number for my apartment. "I swear there isn't any reason for you to be mad."

"Who said I was mad?" I asked as I waited for Dallas to pick up on the other end of the phone. "Why should I be mad that you've probably been planning something like this from the moment you knew Drake was going to ask Lana to marry him but I'm only hearing about it now?"

"Because you and Lana weren't supposed to know about it at all," he muttered half under his breath.

"Yeah, and I would have remained ignorant if I hadn't heard him on the phone with Axton about the party Friday night." Lana glared at him. "And trust me, knowing that you are planning this stupid thing with Axton Cage only makes me more anxious."

Dallas finally picked up the phone. "If this isn't Lana or Harper I'm hanging up," she warned.

"It's me," I assured her. "Did you know anything about the bachelor party this Friday?"

"No way!" she exclaimed. "Why would I fucking know?"

"Because your man is helping plan it with mine."

"Fucking assholes!" she bit out. She and Axton were still holding on even through Dallas's continued insecurities about Gabriella Moreitti and Axton. "He never mentioned it."

"You know what we have to do, right?"

"I'll make the arrangements. I know the perfect club."

"Good. I'll see you in an hour and we can plan it out. I say since the bachelor party is Friday, then so is Lana's." I glanced at my friend and she only nodded.

"I'll see what I can do, but this might be something that will require the redhead's help."

I snorted, knowing by 'redhead' Dallas meant Emmie. Those two had become friends during the time Lana's family had stayed on the East Coast right after she had come home from the hospital. "Emmie it is then."

Shane groaned and I knew exactly what he was thinking. For one thing, Emmie probably didn't know about the bachelor party. For another, if Emmie was going to be going to a bachelorette party, then so was Layla.

Nik and Jesse were going to kick his ass!

Shane

With Harper still upset with me, I had to move fast to make other arrangements. I knew that Emmie wasn't going to help me, mainly because when I had begged she pointedly refused. She was helping with plans for Lana's party and to hell with me.

As the days quickly passed, I kept on my toes altering the one party to crashing another. Because Emmie was doing the arranging, I knew that it was going to be almost impossible to get into whatever club she was renting out for the evening. But I had to make sure that we did crash it, or I was going to have three angry men kicking my ass.

Jesse was the first one to call me and nearly rip my head off over the phone. He and Layla were coming out a day earlier than expected just because of the party, and after seeing the way my friend had nearly knocked my brother's head off a few months ago, I was eager to put things right.

"So now you have not only hurt Lana, but you also have my wife going to some party that I know will be hard-core with the way

Em has been dropping hints," Jesse snarled over the phone. "Oh, and Layla is pissed at me! So thanks, bro."

"Why is she mad at you?" I demanded. "You weren't in on this."

"It doesn't really matter to her or Emmie right now. Nik's in the dog house too. Good luck with that, by the way."

Nik had been more pissed than Jesse. "I'm sleeping in a bed that isn't mine!" he raged thirty minutes after Jesse had called me. "You better fucking fix this, Shane. Emmie is making me sleep in your room."

Of course neither one of my band brothers could compare to how furious Drake was. Lana was staying at Harper's until after the party. I was sure that I was going to have the bruise on my chin for a good month. My brother was like a bear with a sore paw the way he was acting. "I told you, no party!" he had yelled right before he caught me off guard with the punch to the face.

It had taken me two hours to calm him down and promise him that I was going to fix it. Still, as pissed as my family was, it didn't come close to how I was feeling. Harper was staying at her apartment with Lana, and I wasn't allowed to visit. I hadn't gone a day without seeing her since we had started dating. There hadn't been a night that she wasn't sleeping in my arms since we first made love.

Now she wouldn't even answer the phone when I called. All my texts received a short, cold reply.

So yeah, I was hauling ass to get things right.

Now, as I stood with eight other rockers outside of the club Axton had been lucky enough to find out from Dallas was the place for tonight's revenge party, I was almost scared at how easy it appeared to be to get in.

The seven foot muscle head that stood in front of the doors to the club had a headset in his ear and spoke to his boss for a moment before stepping aside and letting the nine of us pass. Nik raised his brows at me when I glanced at him.

When I hadn't moved for almost a full minute, Drake pushed past me and into the club. The rest of us could only follow. The corridor was dark. A small light along the floor was the only guide we had so we wouldn't trip over our feet. Loud techno music was playing. Strobe and laser lights were flashing from every angle, giving me a headache despite the years of using those same lights in our concerts.

I had this scary picture in my head of what we were going to find. All the girls with male strippers grinding against them. Harper sandwiched between two guys while they rubbed their junk all over her… My fists clenched at my sides, and I nearly punched a wall as we all increased our speed.

When we reached the bar area that had the dance floor right behind it, we all stopped at the sight that greeted us.

The place was empty.

Except for a bartender behind the bar, the place was completely empty. Drake exploded into a round of viscious curses that no one heard because the music was so loud. I pulled out my phone, hoping beyond hope that Harper would answer me this time when the music was suddenly cut off.

The lights came on and I had to blink a few times before my vision returned to normal. From the top floor of the club stood a group of laughing women dressed in killer club wear. At the sight of Harper standing between Lana and Dallas, my heart flipped over. The look she was giving me told me I was forgiven because the joke was on me.

"So," Emmie called from the second floor. "Have we learned our lesson?"

"Fuck, I love her," Nik muttered under his breath, staring up at Emmie in awe.

Harper

With only about fifteen people in the huge club, it left for lots of dark, quiet corners. I was thinking about taking advantage of one after having spent nearly a week away from Shane.

I had gotten over being mad at him a few hours after our argument. I might have even given in and run back to him then and there. But Dallas, Emmie, and Layla had intervened. We had to teach them a lesson, they told me. Not just Shane, but all of them.

Teach them that we weren't going to put up with something like this without there being consequences.

Because I was feeling so weak, I could only talk to Shane through texts or I would have told him everything.

Now, with Drake and Lana back in each other's arms after nearly a week of separation, I was sure that I wasn't the only one planning on using a dark corner. Grinning at Dallas, I pushed her toward the stairs. "Let's go find our own guys."

"You go," Dallas frowned down at the first floor. Axton and the rest of the members of OtherWorld were laughing and ribbing each other as they chugged down the apple cider, which was the hardest thing on the menu for tonight out of respect for Drake.

I left my friend to her heavy thoughts. Dallas had it bad if she was still with Axton despite all her doubts. I knew she had a lot on her plate at the moment and hoped that she was able to work things out with her relationship so she could deal with all the other things she needed to deal with.

I passed Layla and Jesse at the bottom of the stairs, but they didn't see me. Layla had her legs wrapped around the big man's waist while he had her pushed up against the wall. Grinning, I continued on my way.

As I reached the bar it was to find that Shane had disappeared on me. Frowning, I hopped up onto one of the barstools and asked for a ginger ale from the bartender. Maybe Shane was mad at me.

"Well hello, kitten."

Glancing up, I found Wroth Niall and Zander Brockman standing right beside of me. My mouth dropped open a little when I realized that it had been Wroth that had spoken. Wroth was known as kind of a woman hater. Not that it stopped hordes of females trying to grab his attention. The guitarist not only played like a freaking dream, but he was perhaps the hottest male in the rock world—or so all the tabloids said. I wasn't so sure because Shane had me captivated.

"Hi, guys," I greeted a little hesitantly.

"You have got to be Stevenson's girl," Zander said with a grin. "Now I see why he's been in such a tizzy all day."

I blinked. "Thanks… I think."

"It's kind of crazy to think of that fucker with a steady girl..." Wroth shook his head "...but obviously he has good taste."

My cheeks warmed with a mixture of pleasure and embarrassment. I still wasn't used to compliments from hot guys. "I like to think he does."

I sat there talking to both of the guitarists for a long while. I found they were both kind of charming underneath all of that rocker toughness. Wroth was an ex-Marine, which fascinated me, and I wondered if I could get him to give me an interview for *Rock America*. I liked both rockers a lot and even found myself laughing with them.

When Shane still hadn't appeared, I felt a little deflated and excused myself to the ladies' room.

The bathrooms were at the back of the club, down a hidden corridor. As soon as I turned the corner to the ladies' room, a strong hand wrapped around my waist and pulled me against a hard chest. Startled, I nearly screamed until the familiar, tantalizing smell of Shane's aftershave hit my senses and I melted against him.

I dropped my purse and wrapped my arms around his neck, holding on for dear life. "I thought you were mad at me and you left," I nearly sobbed.

"So now we've both learned our lesson, huh?" he teased before his mouth devoured my own.

I kissed him back, trying to make up for the days we shouldn't have been apart. I was so glad I had worn the little black skirt that Dallas had suggested I borrow from her. Shane wasted no time in pushing it up my hips as he backed me against the opposite wall.

Maybe I should have been worried about someone finding us like this. But I didn't. Shane had brought out the wild side in me. During the last few months, we had made more than a handful of visits to Sensual House, and one of their rooms gave you the experience of having public sex with the one way mirror that took up nearly one whole wall.

Oddly enough, that had been my favorite room to experiment in. It was so naughty watching people walk by the one way mirror while Shane took me against the wall, or on the bed, or any other place in that room. But there had been that safety net of no one being able to see us. I couldn't believe how hard I had come when Shane had taken me against the wall for the first time while I watched a couple stop in front of the wall of the mirror I was looking out of. While the man turned to kiss his girlfriend, I had been filled with a rush that had nearly brought me to my knees as I came around Shane.

A moan escaped me when his fingers slipped under the hem of my panties to find me wet for him. Two fingers thrust into me, and I clenched around them with need.

"I don't think I can be gentle," he growled against my ear, making me shiver in anticipation.

"I don't want gentle. I want it rough. Hard."

"Thank fuck!" Two seconds, that was all he needed to free himself and thrust into me.

Harper

It was Christmas Eve.

Not exactly what I would call an ideal time to get married, but it was what Lana and Drake had wanted, so who was I to judge. I stood in the back of the church in my bridesmaid's dress with Emmie, Layla, and Dallas. We were just relaxing, talking about nothing of any consequence while we waited for the wedding to start.

I was surprised at how calm Lana was. When I had been a bridesmaid for Cecil's niece a few years ago, she had been anything but calm. She had been borderline bridezilla, screaming at everyone for no apparent reason, sweating off her makeup and having to reapply it several times. But Lana was just sitting on the little sofa with her sister beside her, laughing along with everyone else when Emmie made some mouthy comment.

I was curious as to how Drake was taking the small wait before the wedding started. While everyone else was talking, not paying attention to me, I stepped out of our little room and quietly went down the hall to where Shane and his brother were. Before I lifted my hand to knock, I heard Drake.

He wasn't as calm as Lana by a long shot. "What if she decides that she doesn't want to marry me after all? I mean who could blame her? I'm no good for her. She deserves better."

"Of course she does. She deserves a fucking lot better," Jesse said in a hard, cool tone. "But she wants *you*, Drake. Lana loves you, dickhead."

"But…"

Not wanting to hear Drake tearing himself to pieces a moment more, I opened the door without knocking. Drake was pacing, his hands raking through his shaggy hair like a man tormented. Nik and Jesse stood by the window revealing December in New York and the two inches of snow already on the ground. Shane was sitting on the little leather sofa across the room, watching his brother with troubled eyes.

All eyes turned on me when I entered the room. Without even second guessing what I should do, I crossed over to Drake and hugged him tight. After only a small hesitation, he hugged me back. "Lana sends her love. She can't wait to see you and become your wife."

All the tension seemed to evaporate from his body. For a moment his arms tightened around me. "Thank you," he whispered.

With a smile, I stepped back and gave his hands one last squeeze before leaving the room. Back in Lana's room, I went over to her and dropped a kiss on top of her head. "Drake sends his love."

"Is he okay?" Lana asked.

"He's doing better now," I promised.

The church was huge but it was nowhere near full. OtherWorld and a few other rockers were in attendance, but that about summed up the guest list. Linc, Cecil, and a girl that was related to one of the members of OtherWorld were the only normal guest in attendance. Lana's father was sitting in the front row watching with all smiles as Jesse gave Lana away.

The ceremony was beautiful, and I couldn't keep the tears at bay as I watched Drake struggle through his vows as he openly cried. When the minister pronounced them husband and wife, Drake pulled Lana close and kissed her with such love and tenderness that I was sure there wasn't a dry eye in the church.

The reception was just as small as the ceremony had been. Of course there were paparazzi trying to get in, but Emmie had hired security to keep everyone out. My boss had asked me to do an article on it, but I had told him point blank that I wouldn't. Lana and Drake wanted this special day to remain just for them; they didn't have to share it with the world. And I wasn't going to disrespect them by writing about it.

"This is nice," Shane murmured as he pressed his lips to my ear while we danced. "Maybe it will give you a few ideas about your own wedding."

I stilled in his arms. Shocked to the point of being nearly unable to stand up on my own, I leaned into him for support. "W-what?" I managed in a voice that was more than a little squeaky. Marriage hadn't been on my mind. We had only known each other a handful of months. But now that he had put that little bug in my mind, I had all kinds of crazy thoughts flashing through my head!

I felt his lips lift into a smile against my forehead. "Just a thought."

"You're a jerk, you know that?" I closed my eyes, but I couldn't help but smile. "I love you, though."

"I love you more, beautiful."

Shane

Christmas passed with more spirit this year than there had been the year before. Drake and Lana were off on their honeymoon in the Bahamas instead of rehab this time, so we were all breathing a little easier. We were all smiles as opposed to the tension that everyone had been feeling just twelve months before when Lana had announced that she was moving across the country to start a new life that didn't involve Drake.

I got to wake up with Harper in my arms, so I had a reason to be happy no matter what day it was. We shared the morning with my family, who were staying in New York until Lucy had to go back to school after the New Year. Then we went back to Harper's apartment and had dinner with Dallas, Linc, and Cecil.

I liked to think that Cecil and I had become something of friends over the months that I had been with Harper. I knew that Harper thought of him as her only family, so I made sure that we were on good footing. I was sure that the case of fifty year old bourbon I got him for a Christmas present had only cemented our bound. It sure made Harper happy to see her stepdad's eyes light up when he unwrapped the heavy present. Harper was the most important person in my world, second to no one. My goal was to make sure that she always knew how special she was to me.

So when she had to go to Miami for a three day conference, I wanted to go with her. Of course, she didn't think that was a good idea. Since the whole Trey incident, I had been a little overprotective when it came to her job. Following her to interviews, making sure that whomever she happened to be meeting knew exactly why I was there, and probably scaring the shit out of a few people along the way.

Harper's boss loved the fact that I was her boyfriend and had even asked her repeatedly to get me to do an exclusive interview and photo shoot for the magazine. I was all for doing what would give her the push she needed in her career. Harper wouldn't have it though. She didn't want to use our relationship to move up the ladder.

I ended up staying home while she went off to Miami for the conference the second week of January. She had argued and argued, but in the end it had been the promise of a full night at one of our favorite rooms at Sensual House when she got back that had made me back off. I knew that she needed to give the conference her full attention, and that if I were to go with her I would just distract her.

Not that it was a bad thing in my book, but to Harper it was a big deal.

The first night without her sucked.

I was sitting in front of the television flipping through channels, feeling both bored and lonely since Drake and Lana would be gone for at least another week. Harper was supposed to call me after the big dinner with her boss and other higher-ups ended, but I still had at least an hour before I would get to talk to her.

Lucy had been texting me off and on all evening. She had been back to school for a few days now, and she loved the creative writing class her teacher had put her in. The kid had a wild imagination that was for sure. Half the things she wrote about I couldn't determine if it had actually happened or not.

When the doorbell rang I had my mind on half a dozen other things than who could possibly be stopping by unannounced. I was rereading a text from Lucy, laughing to myself as I jumped up off the couch and crossed over to the door. I figured it was Axton, bored now that America's Rocker was over for the season.

If not Axton, then it was Dallas stopping by to pick up something that Harper had left here that she wanted to borrow. It wouldn't be the first time Dallas stopped by out of the blue just to pick up a pair of shoes or a shirt. Sometimes Linc was with her, and I always welcomed spending time with my new muscle headed pal. It didn't bother me that Linc was gay, and now that I knew for sure that he was, I felt a hundred percent better about his friendship with my girl.

The knocking came again before I could reach the door, more insistent this time, and I rolled my eyes. Yup, it had to be Dallas. No one else I knew would be so demanding after only a minute of waiting. I jerked the door open. "Give a man a break, bitch...."

I broke off when I found a girl that looked no more than sixteen or seventeen standing on my door step. With her dark brown hair with golden highlights falling halfway down her back, she looked even younger than I suspected her to be. Eyes that were so familiar I had to blink a few times before I could focus on any other facial feature.

"Do you always greet people like that?" Came the smart ass reply that she'd inherited from her mother.

"Only the ones that annoy the hell out of me," I assured her, leaning against the doorframe. "What do you want, Nat?"

"I need your help..."

Harper

I frowned down at my phone.

Shane wasn't answering. I had been calling for two days now, and he hadn't picked up once since I'd been gone. I would have been worried that something had happened to him if he hadn't answered my texts.

Each reply was the same. He was busy and couldn't answer my calls because he didn't have a free second to talk to me. I was confused as hell. He was free as a bird right now. Emmie didn't have a tour scheduled for at least a few months, and then it was only for two weeks. He didn't have anything music related to deal with, and I knew that he had nothing other than friends and working out to keep him occupied.

When I had called Dallas to ask if she would go over and check on him she had sent Linc. But when Linc had stopped by after work, Shane hadn't been home. Or he at least hadn't answered the door, and Linc said he had knocked for at least ten minutes.

I had even called Emmie, wondering if she had heard from him. She hadn't talked to him in three days, which wasn't like Shane at all. Those two couldn't go more than a day without some kind of communication. Emmie had then called Layla, and Layla said that Lucy hadn't talked to him since the first evening I had left. Their text conversation had suddenly ended, but Lucy hadn't thought anything of it at the time.

I could only come up with one conclusion.

Shane was tired of me and blowing me off.

The longer I thought about it, the more plausible that conclusion felt. Shane was just burnt out on me, had gotten his fill, and now I was getting the brush off. My entire body felt like it was being stabbed with a million little pinpricks at the thought. My heart was cracking with every passing minute, and I was having to fight back tears as I boarded my northbound plane the next morning.

My first thought was to go home and hide under the covers. But the more pain I felt over my breaking heart, the angrier I became. So I gave the taxi driver Shane's address instead of my own. It was late evening and I was dog tired after two sleepless nights and a stress-filled plane ride from Miami. So when the doorman offered me a smile and a "good-evening Miss Jones," I didn't even look twice at him.

I was too mad, too hurt, and still rehearsing what I planned on saying to the fucking rocker that thought I was just going to go away quietly.

When the elevator opened onto Shane's floor, I got off and used the key he had given me months ago. The lights were on in the living room so I knew he was home. I went straight to his room, expecting him to be in the shower. This time of the evening he was probably just getting home from the gym for the second or even third time.

But he wasn't in there.

"Shane!" I yelled his name, knowing that he had to be somewhere in the freaking apartment.

The noise from the guest room made me turn in that direction, and I threw the door open without bothering to knock. The light was on and the bed was a mess. Unless Emmie or one of the others were in town, this room was closed up, the bed always made, and the lights off.

A muttered curse caught my attention and I stiffened. It hadn't been Shane's voice, but a very feminine one. Stomping through the room, I pushed the bathroom door open to find a nearly naked girl standing in front of the shower.

I got a glimpse of long dark brown hair, big eyes, and a gaping mouth before I turned and ran.

Fucking rocker!

Tears spilled from my eyes, and I didn't even know the real reason for them. I didn't know if it was because I was so mad or because I was so destroyed. Stupid, stupid, stupid rock stars!

I tossed my key on the table by the door as I grabbed my overnight bag and slammed the door behind me. How dare he do this to me! How dare he claim to love me one night, then replace me the next! But I should have known better, should have listened to my gut when it had screamed at me to keep Shane Stevenson at a distance all those months ago.

As the elevator came to a stop in the lobby, I scrubbed my hand over my face to get rid of my tears, but more fell. As the doors opened, I moved to get off only to find my way blocked by the man trying to get on...

"Hey, baby..."

I couldn't stop myself. Didn't even have the sense of mind to even try to withstand the urge as I lifted my hand and smacked him across his handsome face.

"Bastard!" I screamed at him. "You didn't have the guts to tell me you replaced me. Couldn't have taken two minutes out of your busy life to let me know that you've moved some slut into your apartment. I should have known better..."

Strong arms wrapped around me, trapping my arms against my sides. Shane's face was a mask of rage as he glared down at me. "What the fuck are you talking about?" he exploded.

"You wouldn't even answer the phone while I was gone. I should have known something was up then."

"I didn't answer the phone because I was busy!" he yelled in my face, his eyes wild as they searched mine. "I had family problems to deal with, dammit."

"I spoke to Emmie yesterday, Shane. There hasn't been anything wrong with anyone in your family." I tried to pull free from him, determined to leave and never look back. I had been such an idiot to think that things could work with this man.

"Fuck this!" He pushed me back into the elevator and punched the button for his floor. "I can't talk to you in the lobby with you screaming at me, Harper."

I struggled to get free. There was no way I wanted to go back into his apartment and face his new fuck buddy. I fought against his hold, my hair smacking him across the face repeatedly as the elevator rose. "Harper, stop it. You're going to hurt yourself, baby."

"Let go of me!" I cried, tears of frustration and humiliation now pouring down my face. "I hate you!"

Even through my struggle, I felt him tense at my words. As soon as the elevator opened on his floor, he tossed me over his shoulder and lifted my overnight bag. He stomped down the corridor and pounded on the door to his apartment when he couldn't pull his key from his jeans pocket without dropping me.

Moments later, the girl from the bathroom opened the door in a towel. I glared at her over Shane's shoulder as he walked into the apartment. "Dammit, Nat!" he exclaimed. "No wonder she's so mad! You can't go around like that."

"I was in the shower!" Nat defended. "She just walked in and then ran off before I could even say a word. This isn't my fault!"

"Put me down!" I beat my fists against Shane's back hard enough that I felt him grunt in discomfort. "Put me down now!"

He ignored me as he continued through the apartment and into his bedroom. The door slammed behind us, and he paused only long enough to lock the door before dropping me on the bed. I bounced twice before I landed on my back, my hair in my face.

I pushed my hair out of my face to find Shane glaring down at me like I was the one in the wrong. "You have absolutely no trust in me do you?" he demanded.

"After the last few days, the answer would be a definite no." I had trusted him wholeheartedly until he had given me a reason not to.

"Natalie isn't who you think she is." He started pacing, shooting me dirty looks each time he passed me. "If you had given me two minutes to explain things to you instead of tearing into me like a wild cat, I would have told you that Natalie is my sister."

I almost snorted in disbelief until I remembered him telling once that he had a half-sister and her name was Natalie. "You said you didn't have anything to do with your sister."

Shane continued to pace. "I never have before. Her mother refused to let Nat or my dad have anything to do with Drake and me when she married him. She hated the thought of Dad having had another family before her. It wasn't until after my mother died that Dad put his foot down and tried to reconnect with us. But by then Drake and I didn't want to play happy family with a guy that hadn't tried to be there for us when we had needed him the most."

I straightened up on the bed, moving so my feet were hanging off the side. Just because the girl I thought had replaced me turned out to be his sister did not mean that I was less angry. "And you couldn't take five minutes to answer the phone and tell me that your sister was staying with you? Or even text me with that news?"

"I've been searching the city for my sister, Harper. I've had to deal with cops and a stepmother that claimed I kidnapped her. If Natalie hadn't shown up to warn me, then it's hard to tell where I would be right now!"

"You had to look for Natalie?"

"No, I had to look for Jenna." He raked his hands through his hair, going back to pacing after only a small pause.

"Who's Jenna?"

"She's my twelve year old sister." Shane grimaced. "I didn't even know she existed. But she knew about me and Drake. She's been watching Drake on America's Rocker, and when her mother pissed her off she ran off to find us. So Stella called the New York cops and they turned up on my door step twenty minutes after Natalie did."

It was a lot to take in, but slowly it all registered. Shane had almost been arrested. If Natalie hadn't been there to explain that he hadn't taken Jenna—that she was still missing—then the cops probably would have taken him in. He had spent that night and all of yesterday looking for Jenna around New York with the cops and Natalie.

Jenna had been found on the subway late the night before. The girl was now on her way back home, but Natalie hadn't wanted to go. She was going to stay in New York with her brother for a while.

Since she was eighteen she could do whatever she pleased, even if her mother had thrown a fit about her oldest daughter's decision.

My chest stopped hurting, but my gut twisted when I realized how big of a mistake I had made. I had accused Shane of something horrible, had hit him, and then to top it off...I had told him I hated him!

Shane

I would admit that not calling Harper had been a mistake. Finding Natalie in my apartment the way she had probably was the nail in the coffin. But I had thought that Harper trusted me more than that. I'd been so caught up in everything else going on with us that I only assumed that she had complete faith in my feelings for her.

I had never been more wrong in my life.

She hadn't trusted me at all. Harper didn't have a shred of faith in me. That knowledge hurt worse than anything ever had before.

After telling her about how crazy the last few days had been for me, she just sat there with her head bowed, and I continued to pace. I wanted to go running, needed the burn of a long hard run to clear my head and ease some of the pain that clenched my heart. Instead, I just watched the woman that owned me, body and soul, tear me apart with her continued silence.

"I'm sorry I hit you," she whispered so softly that I nearly missed it.

I stopped mid-step and turned to face her fully. "Why couldn't you have given me two minutes, Harper?"

A shaky sigh escaped her, and she scrubbed a hand over her still damp face. "Because I was sure that you had tossed me aside. That you didn't want me anymore. One look at Natalie getting in the shower, and I knew that you finally opened your eyes and saw the truth."

"What are you talking about?"

"I'm not beautiful enough to be with you."

Her words were like a stab to the heart, and I fell to my knees in front of her. This time the pain was more intense, more breath-stealing. Because I realized that Harper probably did have some faith in me, but she had absolutely none in herself. I had thought I had set her fears to rest and was sure that I had given her back her self-worth that her mother and stepsister had stolen from her.

And maybe I had for the most part. But there was still a little piece that would always question her hold over me. "What can I do to make you see what I see, Harper? How can I prove to you that you are the most beautiful thing I have ever seen?"

She bit her trembling lip, and I was gutted as a few tears fell down her pale cheeks. "When I'm with you I feel like the most beautiful thing in the world. When you hold me I feel sexy and loved... And I really did trust you, Shane. I *do* trust you. But... I don't... I'm scared that you'll open your eyes one day and wonder why you are with me. I'm terrified that someone with real beauty will catch your eye and..."

My hand covering her mouth stopped the words that were like poison arrows to my heart. "That's never going to happen. There isn't any way that anyone, beautiful or not, will ever be able to catch my eye. Simply because I can't look at another woman. All I see is you, Harper. All I want and will ever want is you. And I will never—never, do you hear me?—wonder why I'm with you because I already know the answer."

I pulled her down onto the carpeted floor in front of me. "I'm with you because there is no one in the world like you. No other girl could ever hold my attention the way you do. You are so smart and so fun to be with. You are quiet and feisty all at the same time, which is completely adorable and incredibly hot. And your beauty, Harper, it goes soul deep."

I cupped her face, wiping away falling tears as they landed on her cheeks with my thumbs. "Maybe one day you will see all of those things. But until you do, I'll just have to remind you every day. I will have to make sure that you are always in my arms so you never doubt again for even a minute that you are sexy and loved, and completely—irrevocably—mine."

A sob escaped her and she threw her arms around my neck. Her lips tasted of her tears as she sought my mouth in a kiss that was healing for both of us. "Don't cry, beautiful. It kills me to hear those little sobs," I whispered when I pulled back a little.

"I'm sorry!" She buried her tear soaked face in my shirt. "So, so sorry. I love you. I love you, Shane."

I let out a long, relieved sigh. "When you said you hated me…" I broke off, my throat choking with tears. Those three words were still echoing through my head, making my gut twist in pain.

"I didn't mean it. I was just so upset." Tear dampened lips kissed over my face. "I could never hate you, even if I really wanted to. Why do you think it hurt so much for me to come home to this? It was ripping me apart, and I attacked before you could defend yourself."

I nodded. "Yeah, I know. It still hurt though, baby. Thinking that I was about to lose you, that ripped me apart."

Tears poured from her eyes faster. "Can you forgive me?"

"I already have."

Harper

I woke with a headache, but Shane's comforting arms were wrapped around me from behind. We had spent the entire night just lying in his bed, holding onto each other and talking. We had fallen asleep in each other's arms in the early hours of the morning, and I had rested peacefully for the first time in days.

Shane groaned in his sleep and then blinked his eyes open when he felt me moving. His eyes were bloodshot, his face still a little pale, and I felt guilt eat at me once more for putting him through the disaster of yesterday. With a sad smile, I brushed a tender kiss over his lips. "I love you."

"I love you too, beautiful."

"Listen… I have to talk to you about something." It was something that should have been discussed the night before, while we were still pouring our very heart and soul out, but I hadn't wanted to argue again.

His eyes narrowed. "What now?"

"I know that you got me the job with *Rock America*. I know that you had Emmie take a look at my portfolio and ask to send work my way." At the time my boss had let those little facts slip out, I'd still been upset because Shane hadn't called me back while I was in Miami. I was livid and it had been one of the reasons I called Emmie.

Shane grimaced. "I just asked her to make a few phone calls. To ask them to look over your work and see if they could possibly be interested. That's all, Harper. The fact that they ended up giving you a full-time position is all on you. You showed them how talented you are."

I sighed. "Yeah, Emmie made me see that when I called her. I just wanted to say… Thank you, Shane. For helping me. For loving me… But mostly for not giving up on me yesterday when it would have been easier to just tell me to go to hell."

"Telling you to go to hell would have just sent me there too, baby." He pulled me against him, tucking my head under his chin. "One day you'll realize that I can't live without you, and that's the day I'm going to put a ring on your finger."

My heart stuttered in my chest, making it hard to breathe for a moment. And then I was on top of him, kissing him anywhere I could reach. "Don't give up if it takes longer than expected," I begged as I kissed across his hard stomach.

Rough fingers tangled in my hair. "Never going to happen."

When I reached the fly on his jeans, I carefully released him and took him into my mouth without bothering to push the material off his hips. He shouted my name, his fingers tightening in my hair. "Fuck! That feels so good."

The taste of his desire exploded on my tongue, and I moaned at getting a fix for my biggest addiction. I took him deep, not even gagging as I swallowed the head of his dick. I could feel his release nearing as I stroked his shaft and sucked on the tip.

He moved so fast I was still licking the taste of him from my lips when he tore my skirt off and ripped my panties in his urgency to become one with me. The first thrust made me see stars. It felt so good to have him inside of me. "I love you, Shane!" I cried as my orgasm rushed to consume me.

"Love you, baby."

It was a while before we left the bedroom.

I showered and tossed on my robe over my bra and panties and headed into the kitchen for a strong cup of coffee. Shane was already there throwing together a late lunch for us. His sister sat at the island watching him while he moved around humming.

My cheeks heated when Natalie turned to look at me as I entered the room. I bit my lip, knowing that I owed the girl an apology for acting so stupid the day before. "Hi, Natalie."

The girl grinned. "Hey, Harper."

"Look, I'm sorry about yesterday…"

Natalie raised a hand, cutting me off mid sentence. "No, don't. You don't have to apologize to me. I would have definitely reacted the same way if it had been me in your shoes."

"Natalie is going to be staying a few more weeks, baby." Shane placed a cup of coffee down in front of me, along with a plate of sandwiches and some baked chips. "She's thinking of staying in New York."

"That's good. You can get to know your brothers better."

"Actually, I had a crazy idea…" Shane grasped my hand, giving it a tight squeeze. "What if…you moved in here full time and Natalie took your room at Dallas and Linc's."

"I…" I saw the light in his eyes and knew that he was asking for something that he wasn't sure he could put into words. This was the first step, the step he needed me to take to get us on the road to our future. I smiled up at him. "We can talk to Dallas and Linc about it. But as long as she can pay her third of the rent, there isn't going to be a problem."

"I won't have a problem paying my share," Natalie assured me. "The trust fund Drake and Shane started for me will be able to cover that and college in the spring."

I blinked, surprised by the girls words. Shane and his brother hadn't wanted anything to do with their father, and by default Natalie. But that hadn't stopped them from taking care of their sister.

I felt my heart fill with such love I was sure it was shining in my eyes.

"If we had known about Jenna she would have had one too," Shane told his sister. "I'll have Emmie set one up."

"Were you telling the truth, Shane?" Natalie asked. Her eyes, so like her brothers', were sad. "Can Jenna really come and stay on weekends?"

"If Stella allows it." Shane shrugged. "I can't force her hand, Nat. But as determined as Jenna seems, I'm sure she will get her way in the end."

I picked up my cup of coffee, hiding my grin behind the rim. "Sounds like Jenna is a lot like her big brother."

Shane

I parted ways with my brother at the airport.

For two weeks we had been on tour on the West Coast. I wanted to go home, but I wasn't done in California. So I told Drake I would see him in a few days and watched as he boarded a plane that would take him back to New York and Lana.

Jesse, Nik, Emmie, and Mia had already left for Malibu. Normally, if I was staying on the West Coast, I'd just go home with Emmie and Nik and crash in my old room. But I wasn't sticking around LA for them. I had other things I needed to take care of.

Important things.

Harper had been in LA for more than a week now. She was working on the cover for the latest issue for *Rock America*. She had come far with her carrier over the last six months, and with the editor of photography retiring in a few more months, the rumors spread like wild fire that she was up for the job.

I took a taxi to *Rock America's* headquarters, anxious to see my girl after being without her for two full weeks. The last time Demon's Wings had gone on tour, she had come along with us, having been assigned the job of covering the entire tour. That had been the most fun I ever had on a tour in my life.

Traffic was a bitch and my legs were twitching by the time the driver pulled up in front of the magazine's building. I tossed cash at the driver and grabbed my duffle bag, the only luggage I had even bothered to take with me on the tour this time. Fifteen minutes of talking my way through security and I was on the elevator up to the executive offices.

I had to keep myself from jogging down the corridor and bit my lip to stop myself from calling out Harper's name as I searched for the office she had been given for the week as she tried out the possible new position.

At nearly twenty three, she would be the youngest editor on staff. I knew that it was going to mean she had to relocate, and I wasn't against the idea. I had already asked Emmie to start looking for a house.

A vision in pale pink cashmere stepped out of an office ahead of me in the corridor, and my heart stopped for a moment. Oxygen was trapped in my chest, and it took all my willpower not to run and tackle her. My duffle fell to the floor.

"Beautiful..."

The words had come out a whisper, but Harper's caramel head snapped up as if I had yelled it at her. Violet eyes darkened to indigo, and a smile lit up her beautiful face. She had on three inch spiked heels, but that didn't seem to bother her as she dropped the stack of pictures in her hands and ran toward me.

Her lips met mine and I devoured her.

"What are you doing here?" she demanded, breathless. "You said you had to go straight home after the tour."

I dropped another kiss on the tip of her nose. "Don't you know by now that you *are* home, baby? Wherever you are, that's where my home is." At one point it had been Emmie that was home for me, but now it was Harper.

Her eyes glazed over with tears, and she blinked rapidly to keep them at bay. "I love you."

"I love you, Harper." My head turned when I noticed a few people had come out of their offices to watch us. I ignored them. "How much longer do you have?"

"I was just taking the prints to my boss. Then I'm finished for the day." She glanced down at the mess she had made when she had carelessly tossed the pictures she'd been carrying. "It might be a little longer now. I have to put these in order again."

I was reluctant to leave her, but I had a few things to get ready. "Okay, then. You do what you have to then meet me at the hotel."

"Okay." Her bottom lip pouted out. "I won't be long."

Grinning, I bent and sucked that lip into my mouth. "Take your time, beautiful."

I wasted no time getting back to the hotel I had insisted on paying for that Harper would stay in for the week. I grabbed a copy of her room key and headed upstairs. From the tour bus I had called ahead to make sure that everything I needed was already waiting in her room for me.

I spent thirty minutes getting the room just the way I wanted it before taking a two minute shower. By the time I was dressed, there was a knock on the door and I opened it to find room service with the champagne and strawberries. I gave the man a huge tip and rushed him from the room. Harper wouldn't be much longer.

Now all I had to do was wait.

Harper

The last week had been bitter sweet. And now I was at a crossroads. I left my boss' office with my head clouded.

After seeing the cover for the next month's issue for the magazine, I had been offered the job dreams were made of. Of course that meant relocating to California permanently. I didn't know if I was ready for that. After all, I had a great life in New York. Cecil was there, and so were Linc and Dallas.

Shane.

Most importantly Shane. I didn't think I could live that far from the man that had become as much a part of me as another limb. So of course I was conflicted when I left the office. I was still debating the pros and cons when I stepped off the elevator and walked toward my hotel room.

I had argued with Shane for all of an hour over the room. I didn't want him to pay for it and had planned on staying somewhere else that didn't scream over-the-top. But he had kissed me into submission until I agreed, and then he had stepped onto a plane that took him away from me and off on tour.

I used my key card to open the door to my luxurious suite. The room was in complete darkness, and I reached for the light switch.

"Shane?" I called out. Maybe he had gone to Malibu to visit with Layla and Lucy for a while...

The scent of roses filled my nose as I took a few steps into the room. My eyes caught the trail of red, white, and pink rose petals, and my heart twisted with love. I followed the trail, careful not to step on the delicate flower petals. When I reached the bedroom it was to find the room transformed into something from a romance novel.

The room was lit with tiny little candles. An ice bucket with a bottle of expensive Champagne. Rose petals scattered over the king sized bed... And in the center of the bed a tiny velvet box.

I swallowed hard around the sudden tears in my throat.

He hadn't given up. I thought maybe he had. It had taken me so long to fully trust that I was everything he needed. For me to truly see that I was beautiful in every way. When I finally had, I was sure that it was too late. Shane loved me, but I had put him through so much I was sure marriage wasn't something he wanted with me anymore.

On trembling legs, I crossed over to the bed and snatched up the velvet box. My fingers were shaking as I opened the lid.

It was empty!

I fell to my knees as tears poured down my face.

"Hey, now." Strong arms wrapped around me as I felt Shane kneel behind me. His strong chest pressed against my back, and I leaned my head on his shoulder. "You aren't supposed to cry."

"I want the ring!" I sobbed.

Warm lips pressed against my temple. "It's yours, baby. It's right here in my hands." He turned me effortlessly in his arms until I was facing him. "See?" He lifted my left hand and slipped the ring onto my finger but didn't release my hand.

Instead, he lifted it to his lips and tenderly kissed my fingers. "Will you marry me, Harper?"

I swallowed another sob and nodded. "Yes."

His smile was breathtaking. Blue-gray eyes alight with happiness in the candlelight of the room. "I love you, Harper." He kissed me so tenderly and a few more tears escaped my closed eyes. "I want that Carl and Ellie love affair."

"Yes, we will have that. Always."

"When?" I frowned in confusion and he laughed. "When will you marry me?"

"Tonight. Tomorrow…" My mouth snapped shut. I had to give my boss my answer by tomorrow. Was I going to accept the job now?

Shane saw the uncertainty in my eyes. "What is it?"

"Rex offered me the job. It's mine if I want it… But…"

His eyes brightened even more, if that was possible. "That's fantastic, beautiful! I knew they would give it to you."

"That means living here, Shane. What about Drake and Lana? Dallas? Natalie?" Shane's sister had become a big part of our lives. Both of them had. I enjoyed the weekends that Jenna got to spend with us back in New York.

"There are planes, baby. And phones. And all kinds of other ways to communicate with them. Besides, this is your dream job. They will all understand."

"You would really relocate for me? Just like that?"

Shane rolled his eyes. "Of course I would, crazy girl. Just like that."

My heart turned to liquid and I pushed him back onto the floor. "Start planning the honeymoon."

"Baby, I've been planning the honeymoon since I met you."

Coming Soon By Terri Anne Browning

The Rocker Who Holds Her (Nik)
The Rockers' Babies
The Rocker Who Wants Me (Axton)

Playlist

"We Fall Apart" by We As Human
"Never too Late" by Three Days Grace
"Be Somebody" by Thousand Foot Krutch
"All I Need To Know" by Thousand Foot Krutch
"Already Home" by Thousand Foot Krutch
"If I Didn't Have You" by Thompson Square
"Everything Has Changed" by Taylor Swift (featuring Ed Sheeran)
"Miracle" by Shinedown
"I'll Follow You" by Shinedown
"Something More" by Secondhand Serenade
"Addicted" by Saving Able
"Brave" by Sara Bareilles
"Never Stop" by Safety Suit
"Your Guardian Angel" by The Red Jumpsuit Apparatus
"Goodnight Kiss" Randy Houser
"Let Her Go" by Passengers
"Still Into You" by Paramore
"No Matter What" by Papa Roach
"I Wont Give Up" by Jason Maraz
"The Promise" by In This Moment
"Beautiful With You" by Halestorm
"Die Trying" by Art of Dying

CPSIA information can be obtained
at www.ICGtesting.com
Printed in the USA
BVOW06s1828281116
469105BV00019B/310/P